This book is dedicated to my late father Thomas W. Flewharty who gave me a comprehensive list of mystery novels and authors to read when I was a teenager. I am still working on it.

MOLLY FLEWHARTY

SHORT LINE TO DEATH

A NOVEL

Print ISBN: 978-1-54397-394-5

eBook ISBN: 978-1-54397-395-2

CHAPTER 1

The eerie, yellow glow of a sodium-vapor streetlamp lit the grim scene clearly. The dead man lay on his back in the alley next to an overflowing garbage dumpster. A tabloid newspaper folded open to the sports page lay on the ground beside him. Police Chief Billy West knelt beside the body with Officer John Smithfield looking over his shoulder. "Well, I'll be damned. It's Bart Grickly." Billy sighed and shook his head in disbelief. He was thankful it was a few minutes past 4:00 a.m. so no nosy citizens of Cross Keys, Pennsylvania, were likely to be passing by.

"You have been trying to get him for years, Chief!" Officer Smithfield said. "Congrats!" He was the most recent and the youngest addition to the Cross Keys' police department and had discovered the body on his routine survey of town. It was his first major crime scene.

Billy glared at the rookie. "Jesus, Smithfield, 'congrats'?"

"Yeah, I mean he's a big catch."

1

"Well, we didn't exactly catch him," he said as he stood up. "Looks to me like he was strangled."

"I mean he *was* scum, sir. It's good to have him finally off the streets and..."

"I think you are slandering pond scum, but I appreciate your enthusiasm," he said as the ambulance, a state police car and the county medical examiner drove up. "Why don't you run over to the diner and get us some coffee. We're going to be here for a while."

"Yes, sir."

"And Smithfield..."

"Sir?"

"Good work on finding the body."

* * *

Leaning back in his favorite Adirondack chair, Tom Firemark surveyed the canopy of stars through binoculars. Occasionally, he woke early to survey the night sky and enjoy the predawn silence from his back deck. He had built his small timber-frame house himself, after a lengthy search for an appropriate site. The house sat on top of a hill with no neighbors within a mile, just a view of the village of Cross Keys and the Delaware River valley lying beyond a field of dairy cows.

Tom heard the distant sound of sirens and noticed the flashing red lights of emergency vehicles in the middle of town, so he aimed his binoculars in their direction. Something really strange must have happened to create this kind of commotion in Cross Keys at this hour, he thought. He could see the police cars clearly, but they blocked the view past them. He resumed his stargazing until the sky began to lighten with the rising sun. After putting his binoculars away, he grabbed his keys and walked to his Jeep. He reflexively held the door wide and stood back so Freddy could jump in. He sighed and shook his head wondering at his own behavior. Freddy had been dead for two months and he still could not get used to the idea. He looked for the old dog to be just behind him, wagging his tail. He expected to see him in the dog nest he found impossible to throw away or sitting stock-still in front of the window on the lookout for squirrels. He sighed as he got into the car and drove to the Cross Keys Diner.

The diner served plentiful plates of good food at inexpensive prices, making it extremely popular. There was always a wait to be seated on Sunday after church. It was strategically located at the intersection of the two main shopping streets of Cross Keys, High and Franklin. The only traffic light in the town was located at the intersection and was known as the Cross Keys Light. Not long ago, it had been the only traffic signal in the county.

Built in the 1940s, the exterior of the diner was a dull silver metal facade with rounded corners, giving it a bullet-shaped appearance. It was topped with its name on a red, white and blue neon sign. The interior had been refurbished over the years but still retained a vintage feel. There were booths seating two or four and swiveling stools at the counter with all the seats covered in glossy red marbleized vinyl. Movable tables and chairs allowed the rest of the space to be configured to seat as many as needed. On the front edge of the counter, the diner's famous Award Winning Homemade Pie of the Day was prominently displayed in all its glory on a pedestal under a protective, glass cake cover. Nobody knew for sure what *award* they had actually won, but the pies were generally considered to be excellent.

"Good morning, Tom. You're up early today." May beamed brightly at him. She smoothed her red serving smock, which had her name tag surrounded by a half dozen turtle pins on the left-hand side, and tucked the sides of her abundant blond hair behind her ears. She poured his coffee and juice while he bought a newspaper from the machine in the foyer.

Even though she saw Tom almost daily, she always felt a flutter or excitement when he walked into the diner. It was not simply his rugged good looks: he also radiated a calm strength and self-confidence that was especially attractive. He was over six feet tall with a lean, athletic build. He dressed casually, most often in jeans and a button-down shirt with the sleeves rolled up or a short-sleeve polo shirt. His thick dark brown hair had a touch of gray at the temple. Expression lines surrounded his mouth and brown eyes and deepened when his mischievous grin appeared.

"Your usual?"

"Yes, thank you, May," said Tom as he sat at the counter.

"Did you see all the commotion behind the Tickity?"

Tom put down the paper, "No. I was awake and heard the sirens. Thought I would come in early to find out what happened. I figured Billy would show up. Do you know what happened?"

May leaned over the counter closer to Tom. "Officer Smithfield said they found a body!" May sounded more excited than appalled. "Pete thinks it was a tourist that got mugged!" She nodded her head in the direction of the kitchen to indicate the cook.

Tom chuckled. "Mugged? I doubt it. But if that's true, feathers will fly at the next council meeting. So, you don't know who it was?"

"No, but I guess we'll find out from the source," May said as Chief Billy walked in. "Oh my, he looks hungry. I better hide the pie or none of my other customers will get any. It's apple today, by the way." May walked to the end of the counter.

"Good idea. If he's up at this hour, he'll definitely be hungry. When we go fishing, he has two egg sandwiches and a box of donuts before we get out of the car."

"I heard that," Billy said with a tired but pleasant expression on his face. "Hey, May, just ignore him. I'm a hardworking public servant looking for a warm meal after a long night's work. So can I get some service here?"

"Yeah, yeah. Just hold your horses," she said grabbing a pot of coffee.

"Good morning, Tom," Billy said has he sat on the stool next to Tom. "I will take my usual with extra bacon, thank you, May." She poured him a mug of coffee and put in his order.

May adored Billy as he always brightened her day with some silly comment or exaggerated compliment. Although not as handsome as Tom, she considered Billy an attractive man. He was of average height and weight, with incredibly bright blue eyes and regular features set in a flawless peaches-and-cream complexion. His light brown hair was thinning, so he kept it cut short. Billy had returned to town from the Philadelphia police department when the police chief position had become available five years ago.

Billy looked from one to the other and grinned. "I know you two are dying to know what happened last night."

"So? Don't keep us in suspense. What happened on the mean streets of Cross Keys?" May asked.

"Bart Grickly was discovered dead in the alley. The death was *not* from natural causes."

"My, my, that is news! Well, that will do a whole lot to clean up our little corner of the world," May said. "My Ted says the Lyon police consider him a one-man crime wave. Or considered, I guess I should say."

Billy nodded. "That is correct. An extremely slippery one-man crime wave."

"Well, there aren't a great many employment opportunities in this area, especially if you have a snake tattoo running from your neck to your shaved head. At least he was an entrepreneur. If not the most desirable one," Tom observed.

"Yeah. He was ambitious enough. Had a smorgasbord of illegal activities." Billy shook his head as he put five teaspoons of sugar and a dollop of cream into his coffee.

"How was he killed?" asked Tom.

"Well, it's too early for anything official, and you know I can't give out information on an active investigation. But I will say the cause of death was obvious," the chief said as he stirred his coffee. "This is going to be a hard one to solve, unless I find a witness. Bart had many enemies, I'm sure."

"Well, maybe you'll get lucky."

"Billy is always lucky," said May as she put their breakfast plates down. "But I hate to think what folks will say once they know there's a killer on the loose."

"Especially in tourist season," Tom added.

"Do you want pie, Billy?"

Billy looked insulted. "Of course. It's apple, right?"

May nodded.

"A nice big piece with vanilla ice cream."

"Murder increases your appetite, huh? And I didn't think it could get any bigger," Tom quipped.

CHAPTER 2

Madeline Williams woke with a start to the sound of birds tweeting. She could not believe the racket. She had been living in Cross Keys for almost four months, and this was the first time she had heard so much bird noise. Of course, unseasonably warm weather had allowed her to sleep with the window cracked open for the first time. Apparently, the birds had woken up now that spring was undeniably beginning and wanted the entire world to be awake also. She was accustomed to the early-morning noises of Manhattan, including garbage trucks, car alarms, people yelling, alley cats howling and horns honking, but she was unprepared for loud chirping. Country living was definitely going to take some additional adjustments she had not anticipated.

She lay in bed and marveled at the different bird songs. She smiled at the happy sound, but then she looked sadly at the empty space in the bed where her husband should be. Wildlife was not the only change in her life to concern her. She had lost her husband to a younger woman. John had cheated on her and left her. She had been completely unaware there was a problem, as everything in their lives seemed to be the same as it always had been. Maybe that had been the problem.

Her marriage of thirteen years had started out as a wonderfully compatible and passionate relationship. They had shared a condo in Manhattan and enjoyed all the benefits of living in the city. They had decided early on that parenthood was not for them and had traveled and happily spent time alone together. They had been close in every way and enjoyed each other's company. As a result of their closeness, she had let many of her other friendships dwindle. After John had revealed he was in love with some young woman he'd met in the gym, he moved out, leaving her deeply hurt and alone. She had no close family, and so after John left her, she'd discovered she had her career as head of the accounting department of a small investment-management firm and her work friends but little else.

She could not figure out what had gone wrong, and John refused to discuss it. She was stunned into an emotionless state, living each day in a fog but trying desperately to appear as if nothing was wrong. She had no idea what to do, and so she did nothing, burying herself in work so there was no time to think about the situation.

Then after three months, he had wanted to reconcile. Apparently, Crystal had found another younger and richer boyfriend and had no use for John any longer. She'd abruptly tossed him out of her small apartment. He'd shown up at home and expected Madeline to be happy he had returned, as if he had been on an extended business trip. She wasn't. He told her how sorry he was and vowed he would never leave her again. The numbness seemed to drop from her, and she became angry. She knew this was an empty promise. Her answer was to file for divorce the next day. It had been difficult because she still loved him, but his betrayal and apparent belief she would take him back no matter how callously he'd behaved meant she could never take him back. That was six months ago. To her it had felt like a lifetime.

During John's absence, she'd received news of an unexpected bequest. A registered letter informed her she had inherited her great-aunt Inez's house and its contents in Cross Keys, Pennsylvania, including her 1980 Cadillac Sedan DeVille. She had fond memories of spending a large part of many childhood summers in Cross Keys with her grandmother and great-aunt. She recalled playing with neighborhood kids, riding bikes all over town, going to the county fair, swimming in the Delaware River, horseback riding and eating homemade ice cream. And the house itself had been a great place to play, with seemingly endless hidden nooks and secrets. Inez had never married and had lived in the house most of her adult life, operating a beauty parlor on the first floor. Over the years, after her grandmother died, Madeline had lost touch with Aunt Inez. The yearly Christmas cards were their only contact, but even that had been sporadic on Madeline's part. She was surprised and moved that her relative had thought to give her the house.

It was a large Victorian structure built in the late 1800s, standing three stories high, with a sizable covered front porch ending with a gazebo on one side and a turret rising from the opposite corner. It needed some minor repairs but had been generally well maintained. It was painted a pale sherbet yellow with light blue-and-green gingerbread trim. The house was the largest in a quiet residential neighborhood of treelined sidewalks and neatly maintained houses and yards, just a short two blocks east of High Street.

She loved the house and the historic town, which was sandwiched between the Delaware River and the last bit of the Pocono Mountains, at the very tip of the northeastern corner of Pennsylvania, an hour and half drive from Manhattan. Cross Keys had been founded in the middle of the 1700s, and it had grown steadily. In its prime, it had been the favorite summer residence of the more notorious and, therefore, less socially acceptable rich and famous people of the day from New York City.

To keep things amicable until the divorce became final, she'd allowed John to live in the apartment while she moved temporarily to Cross Keys and commuted every day into Manhattan on the bus. The bus stop was within walking distance of the house. The two-hour commute each way was a big change from her ten-minute subway ride to the office, but it was only temporary. With any luck, once the apartment was on the market, they would sell it quickly, divide up their assets and she could find a new place in the city and restart her life. At least that was the plan. But the plan or rather the lawyers seemed to be moving exceedingly slowly.

Her soon-to-be ex-husband would call her and insist they get together to talk about the details of their divorce. They met in the city for lunch a few times. At first, she felt sad when they met, remembering all the good years they had spent together. But he'd changed, and it was almost as if she didn't know him at all. He was clearly trying hard to look younger than his forty years. He had dyed his hair a lighter color, bought new clothes more suitable for a younger man, had an ear pierced and decorated his arms with several tattoos. He had always been tall, dark and handsome in her eyes. Now he looked pathetic. She had her attorney take over, so she would not have to see him again.

She sighed heavily and rolled out of bed. Coffee and breakfast at the diner beckoned. She walked into the bathroom and stepped on the scale. "Ugh," she said out loud as the number was not a good one. Her weight-loss regime was not going well. Since the separation, her diet of comfort food had added fifteen pounds to her short frame, and the long commute had not helped. There was no time for exercise, and by the time she got home, cooking a healthy meal wasn't an option, so she ate takeout or microwave dinners.

After showering, she glanced in the mirror. No one would ever describe her as beautiful, but her regular features and bright green eyes made her face attractive. She brushed her stylishly cut brown hair, put on mascara and got dressed.

During the weekends, she always had a late breakfast at the diner. It was a luxury to indulge in a large breakfast and linger over coffee. She always liked to sit in a booth for two with a window looking out on Franklin Street and the library lawn.

The public library, a tall white structure, was across from the diner and was surrounded by a large lawn which served as a park, with wooden benches and seasonal plants and decorations provided by the Society for the Preservation and Beautification of Cross Keys, or the Society of Pretentious Busybodies of Cross Keys as some people referred to them.

May welcomed Madeline with a smile, a cup of coffee and a glass of orange juice. "I guess you know what everybody in town eats," Madeline said.

The waitress giggled. "Yes. I think I know more about many people than I need to. I could write a book that would curl your hair. You want your usual?"

"No," she said as she studied the menu. "I think I'll have number three today."

"I guess you're hungry. That's two eggs, two pancakes and two strips of bacon with home fried potatoes and toast. Can I interest you in a side of grits or a piece of pie?"

Madeline laughed. "I'm not *that* hungry. Speaking of gossip, anything new today? I depend on you for all the local news."

May nodded. "As well you should. As a matter of fact, there is big news today. One of the less respectable people in the area was found dead this morning in the alley behind the Tick-Tock Lounge." May leaned closer and lowered her voice. "Probably murdered," she said with raised eyebrows and nod of her head.

"That certainly is big news. Who was it?"

"Bart Grickly, a local criminal."

"And I thought this was a happy little town."

"Yeah, it's happy enough, but bad people are everywhere these days."

"I guess so." Madeline pensively sipped her juice and wondered if a security system for the house might be a good idea. She had never considered the need for one. "I thought it was extremely safe here."

May gave her a reassuring smile. "Don't worry, honey. It is safe enough for regular folks. We have very little crime. I don't remember the last time we had a murder."

After breakfast, Madeline did errands around town. The buildings along High Street were restorations and preservations of original structures. The shops catered mostly to the tourist trade and included several antique stores, a jewelry shop, a magic and toy store, an arts and crafts shop and a women's clothing shop. For residents, there was a hardware store, a bakery, a drug store, the post office and a food market. She spent some time talking to Bob Griffin, one of the antique shop owners, about helping her sort through the house and remove items. The house was completely furnished; in fact, it was overstuffed with furniture and bric-a-brac. She had not had the time or inclination to change anything. Her life had been in enough turmoil, and as it was, the house reminded her of happier times.

Later that afternoon as the sunlight faded and the temperature became colder, she started a fire in the fireplace and made a cup of tea. The sap in the pine logs popped, sending sparks flying like miniature fireworks. Sitting in front of the fire all alone made her feel gloomy and isolated. It might be temporary, but it was a big adjustment to have left the city and her husband to live in a small town where she knew no one well.

It had taken Madeline almost a month to become adjusted to her new schedule: waking before dawn, commuting by bus, working all day and finally arriving back home with little time or energy to do more than heat up dinner, watch a little TV and fall asleep. Then doing it all over again the next day. The weekends were taken up with errands to run and chores to do and sleep to catch up on. Sunday night seemed to appear in the blink of an eye, while the workweek lasted an eternity.

One coworker had asked her how Pennsylvania was, and she had replied, "Dark." It was dark when she got up and dark when she got home. She was anxiously awaiting warmer weather and Daylight Saving Time.

CHAPTER 3

During her weekends in Cross Keys, Madeline had discovered a charming restaurant and bar within easy walking distance from her house. The Opossum was tucked behind the west side of High Street on Buckeye Alley, which ran parallel to High. The bar had been in existence in one form or another since the late 1800s. Everyone knew it by its big wooden sign, which hung from a pole jutting out over the alley. The sign did not have the name of the bar on it but instead showed a smiling opossum hanging by its tail from a tree, holding an overly full beer mug with the foamy head spilling over the frosty sides. When there was a stiff breeze, the sign swung with a persistent squeak.

The bar area was very cozy, with dark wood paneling and a stone fireplace large enough for a short adult to stand in. The long dark wooden bar was highly polished from years of use, and the barstools were comfortable, with worn leather seats and backs. A large brass-framed mirror hung over the back bar. On either side of the fireplace, banquettes with tables and chairs allowed for adjustment to any size group, and a small number of tables filled the center of the room. A larger dining room was further back through an arched doorway. The room had antique sconces on the wall that threw out a dim light and gave it an enigmatic atmosphere.

The place was not known for its cuisine, which was basic bar food. The house specialties were the Opossum Burger and the Spaghetti and Opossum Balls, which were not actually made from opossum, although some people had expressed their doubts. During the summer, Friday and Saturday nights were busy when weekenders, seasonal renters and vacationers swelled the town's population. During the winter, locals kept the businesses in town going.

Every time Madeline entered the bar, she smiled. She loved the look and feel of the old place, and she felt comfortable sitting at the bar alone. She had started coming in most Saturday evenings and eating her dinner while sitting at the bar. She had avoided any lengthy conversations with other regular customers, since she did not feel like introducing herself and explaining why she was eating dinner alone in a bar on Saturday night.

However, she did enjoy talking with the owner of The Opossum, Tom Firemark. The conversation was never serious or incredibly personal, just friendly banter. And it was a bonus that she thought Tom was handsome and she had managed to find out he was not married and was straight. He had a good sense of humor and seemed intelligent and kind. Madeline would not have been surprised to learn that he was considered the most eligible bachelor in Cross Keys. His good looks and allegedly storied past made him interesting to both the young and impressionable and the old and jaded. But he had managed to avoid the more persistent and rapacious women who pursued him. He was hard to catch. He was very careful to keep his romantic life as private as possible, but there was always speculation.

There were only three full-time employees at The Opossum, with college students and other part-time help hired during the busy season. Adam Marshall manned the bar and served as the manager if Tom was not around. He was young, extremely tall and so thin that Madeline thought he almost disappeared when he turned sideways. He had long brown hair pulled back into a ponytail and the remains of acne scars on his face and neck. He was certainly not handsome, but he had a brilliant ear-to-ear grin and a charming manner. He was unfailingly welcoming to Madeline from the moment she first started going to the bar.

Debby Warsawski was the waitress, and she also did about any job that needed to be done, from backup cook to bartender to bouncer. She was a curvy, muscular woman in her thirties. Her face reminded Madeline of Betty Boop, with large expressive eyes and small well-shaped lips. She had a seemingly endless string of boyfriends and male cousins whom she gently cajoled into doing repairs around the old building. Tom never had to worry about finding a plumber or electrician for an emergency repair.

The cook was a mystery man. Madeline had never heard him referred to as anything but *Cook*, and she had never seen him. He stayed in the kitchen. Madeline hoped he was not offended by the comments regarding his abilities and mentioned this to Debby. Debby told her that, despite all the jokes, most people ate all of their food and were regular customers.

"Good evening, Madeline." Tom gave her a big grin. From their conversations, and the fact she spent Saturday nights by herself in the bar, he had easily concluded that she was lonely, had been deeply hurt by her estranged husband and was trying to figure out how to start over. He knew firsthand that starting over was never easy.

Madeline had told him about her inheritance of the house her great-aunt had lived in. He had known her aunt as he would any long-standing resident of Cross Keys; they were not friends but passing acquaintances. She had been a well-respected member of the community. The house was a true historic gem. He was glad Madeline had inherited it, as she seemed to understand its worth.

Without being asked, he placed a vodka martini in front of her. "Thank you," she said and smiled at him as she took a sip. "You know, I have been meaning to ask you something."

"Sure. What is it?" He smiled at her but looked uneasy. He was concerned she might have a personal question, and he was not interested in a flirtation with anyone at the moment.

"Why don't you have a signature Opossum cocktail?"

He laughed. "I never thought about it. The burger and spaghetti seemed like enough opossum-related items. What would you suggest?"

"I don't know. Maybe something vodka-based in blue or even violet. I bet the tourists would like it."

Tom looked thoughtful. "Maybe so. What would I call this concoction?"

"I did a little research with Mr. Google, as my older friend at work calls it. Male opossums are called jacks, and females are called jills. Maybe two in different colors called the Jack and the Jill?"

"Well, those sound like children's drinks. I don't serve children vodka-based cocktails. The authorities frown on that," he retorted.

"How narrow-minded of them. But I see your point. How about The Happy Opossum?"

"I guess I need to think about this signature-cocktail concept. I can canvass the other patrons. I'm *sure* they will have opinions," he said as he moved down the bar to serve other customers.

Tom looked around as the door opened, and Billy walked in. He was not wearing his uniform but was dressed in jeans, a navy blue turtleneck and a worn leather motorcycle jacket. He sat on the stool next to Madeline.

"Are you off duty?" Tom asked.

"No, I'm undercover," Billy said sarcastically as he waved his bandaged hand in the air.

"Madeline, do you know Billy West? He is our chief of police."

"No. Pleased to meet you, Billy." Madeline smiled at him.

"Madeline inherited the Henderson house." Billy nodded knowingly. "I have known Billy all my life or at least for as far back as I can remember. What happened to your hand?" Tom asked.

Billy looked crestfallen. "A pony bit me," he mumbled.

"What?" Tom asked, repressing a guffaw and not sure he had heard correctly.

"The White Tail Inn reported their pony, Glen, missing, and at the same time I got a call from Moira that a horse was eating her shrubbery. So, I thought it was Glen, and as my policing duties are varied, I went to get him."

"Glen wasn't happy to see you?" Tom asked with a bemused look.

"Well, here's the thing. It wasn't Glen. It was another pony, and he bit me. Now he's in the firehouse waiting for his owner to pick him up. You know, horses should have to have licenses like dogs do. I hope I don't get rabies or horse fever or something."

"What happened to Glen?" Madeline asked.

"He returned home on his own. Glen tends to roam, but they like to alert me that he's on the loose."

Tom put a Crown Royal on the rocks in front of Billy. "You look like you need this."

Billy nodded in agreement. The bar slowly began to fill up, which meant that Tom had little time to chat with Madeline as he greeted and served other customers. She talked with Billy about his horse problem. "Do you have to find runaway ponies often?"

"No, thank God. And I don't have to deal with wildlife generally. If you have a skunk move in under your porch, you have to call an animal control person, not the police."

"Wow. I never considered that I might find a skunk living under my porch. I know one lives under the library."

"Yeah, I know. He has been moved numerous times but always returns. If one does, I don't advise you try to shoot it with a bow and arrow while you are drinking beer, like my ex-girlfriend's idiot brother."

"I doubt I would think of doing that."

Billy nodded. "I tried to stop him. But he would not listen. He missed and managed to pin one of the skunk's forelegs down. So, he just raised his tail and spun in a circle spraying everywhere. They had all the windows open and the window fan going. The whole place smelled for weeks."

Madeline frowned. "Yuck! Sounds horrible."

Billy nodded. "To put it mildly. And to add insult to injury, I smelled like skunk for days afterwards, no matter how often I showered."

"We called him Pepé Le Pew for a couple of weeks," Adam said as he walked past them.

"Yeah. And the skunk didn't leave. You would think he would realize he wasn't welcome. He moved in under the shed. I named him

Mr. Limpy. Unfortunately, it should have been Mrs. Limpy because she had kits." Billy shook his head.

Madeline tried to look sympathetic and stifled a laugh.

"Oh, go ahead and laugh. I can even laugh about it now."

Moira Kowalski and her husband, Joe, entered the bar.

"Good evening, Moira, Joe," Tom greeted them. "Are you here for dinner or just a drink?"

"Dinner tonight, Tom. For some reason, my Joey loves your spaghetti, even though my homemade sauce is so much better. No offense," Moira said as she gave him a playful glance.

"No offense taken," Tom said as he gave her an intense stare. Moira blushed and looked away. Her bangle bracelets jingled and clanged as she attempted to mount the barstool. After much groaning, wiggling and huffing, she succeeded at last with a final, assisting push from Joe.

Moira was a faded beauty. Madeline thought she must have been very pretty as a young woman, before the onset of her double chin and puffy face and figure. Her eyes were large and hazel, her nose was straight and even regal, and she had a beautiful smile. Her now bright red hair must have been a not too bright red in its natural state, judging from the graying roots. It was laboriously styled in a bouffant flip that was popular in the sixties and now in a modified version was again in style. She always wore six bangle bracelets, which she shook and adjusted constantly, a ring on every finger except her thumbs, and her always immaculate manicure adorned her fingertips with brightly painted talons.

Joe was an average-looking man. Average height, a little above average weight, with hair of a medium light brown color that flopped down over a pleasant but unremarkable face. He was definitely second fiddle to Moira's commanding role.

"Moira, Joe, meet Madeline. She's new in town," Tom said while preparing their cocktails.

"Oh, we know each other from the bus," Moira sighed.

"Yes. Hi, Moira. We made it through another week."

"Oh, heavens yes. It is pure torture." Moira laughed and jingled her bracelets. "By the end of the week, you think you live on that bus."

Suddenly, the door banged open so loudly it made Madeline jump. She looked around to see Roberta Carlson standing with her feet apart and her hands on her hips. A short, wiry, middle-aged woman with a scowl on her unpleasant face, her large pale pink–framed glasses and thin frizzy brown hair did not improve her appearance. She looked ready for a fight, as if she were Wyatt Earp at the OK Corral.

"Uh oh, it's Roberta. Come on, Joey, let's go to the dining room." Joey obediently helped Moira off the stool and followed her into the other space carrying the drinks. Madeline had not heard him speak since the couple had entered the bar.

"Can Moira's husband speak?"

Tom and Billy both laughed. "That's a good question," Billy said.

"I don't think Joe is allowed to have any opinions of his own or speak when Moira is around," Tom explained. "He can be very talkative when you get him by himself and fill him up with port."

Madeline could see Roberta's reflection in the mirror behind the bar and watched as she walked around, obviously looking for someone. She finally came up to the bar and stood next to Billy.

"Hello, Roberta. To what do I owe the pleasure of your visit to my humble establishment?" Tom asked with a blank expression on his face and no enthusiasm in his voice. "Did Agatha throw you out of the Tickity again?"

"Ha ha. I'd rather drink at home with my duller-than-dishwater sister than spend my money with you, Firemark. Plus, I would have to associate with your pitiful clientele. Like this pair. The new boring fat woman from the bus and Billy, our local excuse for a policeman. I'm looking for Tony Fowler. Have you two seen him?"

"No," Tom said.

"Humph. Well, if you see Tony, tell him I am looking for him. He doesn't answer his cell, and I need to speak to him pronto." With that, she turned and gave Billy a withering stare. "Any news on the Grickly case? That bastard owed me money, you know."

"Nothing yet."

"Figures. I doubt you could find your way out of a closet with the light turned off. Keep up the good work, Chief." She turned and stomped out of the bar.

Madeline looked at Tom and Billy, "Yikes! So, what's the deal with Roberta? I thought she was just nasty on the bus."

"She is the meanest woman in town. If not the county and maybe the state," Billy said.

"Has she always been like that?"

"My guess is she was born that way," he said. "But rumor has it she was left at the altar by the love of her life twenty years ago. She has been bitter and nasty ever since. From what I know about her, she lives to cause trouble and make other people miserable."

Tom nodded. "At least, that is what we have heard. I personally have never talked to her long enough to know any more about her."

"I have been unfortunate enough to have to deal with her on town matters. She is a royal pain," Billy added.

"So, you would rather deal with a biting pony?" Madeline asked.

"Oh, you bet! And a mad skunk. Any day of the week."

"She doesn't like you," Madeline said to Tom.

Tom shrugged. "I don't like her either. Lucky for me, she prefers to hang out at the Tickity."

"So, is there really no progress on the investigation?" Tom asked Billy. The chief pushed his empty glass toward him and indicated he wanted a refill.

"Like I said, nothing yet."

"Is that about the man that was found dead in the alley?" Madeline asked.

"Yep. He was killed in the early-morning hours in a town that rolls up the sidewalks by eleven at night. I have no physical evidence and no witnesses. And the more time that passes the colder the trail gets." Billy took a long sip of his drink.

"I bet something will turn up. It will just take time," Tom offered.

"I think I'll have another Opossumtini and an Opossum Burger, please," Madeline said.

"Coming right up!"

"That sounds interesting. What's a Opossumtini?" Billy asked.

Madeline gave Tom a knowing look and he nodded.

CHAPTER 4

Full-time employment options in Cross Keys that paid well were limited. Unless you were a lawyer, a real-estate salesperson, a doctor or had your own business, you were forced to commute to New Jersey, upstate New York or New York City to find work. Some people drove to Port Potter, a small town just over the state border in New York, and caught the commuter train there.

However, the Trusty Transit bus, or the Rusty Bus as the regular commuters called it, remained the most practical option. The bus that served Cross Keys's commuters was not a sleek, modern coach, but more like a large dull green rectangular box with wheels. *Trusty Transit* was painted in large white letters across each side and on the rear of the bus, with the slogan *A Million Miles Safely Traveled* written underneath. The bus looked as if it had traveled most of those million miles.

The two rows of double seats running the length of the interior were old, spotted and cracked brown leatherette with minimal padding left. The bus swayed dramatically during sharp turns, swinging the passengers from side to side as if on a carnival thrill ride.

The route followed by the bus was not the most direct route between Pennsylvania and Manhattan, which would be directly across New Jersey. Instead, it went east, across upstate New York and then turned south through New Jersey. In the morning, after Port Potter, it stopped and filled up with passengers at the Mt. Moore Park and Ride and then went express to Manhattan. In the afternoon, it stopped in New Gottenberg, Madison and Port Potter before the first Pennsylvania stop of Lyon.

There were two early-morning buses and two late-afternoon buses running about an hour apart. Although the bus held fifty-three passengers, a tight-knit group of eleven daily commuters between Pennsylvania and Manhattan dominated the bus, taking seats as a group in the rear where their loud conversation intruded on the peace of all the other passengers.

This clique, known as *the regulars*, was an opinionated group who believed they knew more about running a bus company than the bus company did. This included the route, the weather forecast, traffic, bus maintenance, and driving speed, with fast—but not reckless—being the preferred mode. The schedule was written in stone as far as they were concerned as long as the bus was tardy, but if, by some chance, it was running ahead of time, then the schedule was of no importance at all. They resented anyone who needed to have the underneath luggage area opened, anyone who asked questions of the driver, slow people, old people, people with crying or unruly children, and anyone who purchased their ticket from the driver. In short, they hated tourists, weekenders and the occasional passenger because they added extra time to the already arduous two-hour ride. They hated people who made noise, talked loudly on cell phones (except, of course, if they did) or turned on the reading light in the morning.

* * *

That Monday morning, as usual, Madeline woke before the alarm went off at 3:45 a.m. Even after four months, she was still worried about oversleeping and missing the 5:10 bus. She completed her morning routine, donned her coat and stepped out into the chilly morning air. The solitary walk to the bus stop in front of the library lawn used to make her feel uneasy, but she had gradually grown to enjoy the short walk through the silent town. Many mornings, she was the first to arrive and shared her wait with the fat skunk that lived under the library and foraged around the diner's dumpster.

Slowly and steadily, the other commuters would arrive. The always-wrinkled mess Matt O'Conner, the unnaturally red-headed Moira Kowalski, the rotund Stephen Schmidt, the beautiful Rosemary Lambert, the forlorn-looking Brian Weber, the handsome Tony Fowler, the quiet Elizabeth Rogers, the extraordinarily plain Alice Miller, the buff Jake Kelly, the always loud and nasty Roberta Carlson, and her long-suffering friend, the dollfaced Fern Whitson.

It never failed that Roberta pushed her way to the front of the informal line and barreled up the steps first, dragging Fern with her so they could secure their preferred seats. She would then bark some insult at the bus driver, Dave, as she handed him her ticket. He knew better than to reply. He simply nodded.

Madeline was friendly to everybody, but other than a simple greeting, nobody seemed to want to befriend her. Apparently, they were happy with the group as it was, and no newcomers need apply for admission. The long hours of the commute gave Madeline plenty of time to observe the regulars as she listened to their conversations and watched their interactions. The first thing she noticed was that each person had a seat they normally sat in and a person they normally sat with. How they had arrived at this arrangement she had no idea. But anyone who attempted to disrupt this set seating pattern was dealt with harshly. She found this out the hard way when she had been unaware of this unwritten rule and had sat in a free window seat, which turned out to be next to Roberta's favorite seat. Madeline was told in no uncertain terms by Roberta that she had to *move her fat ass to another seat because that was Fern's seat*, even though Fern was not on the bus that day.

The first row of the clique included Elizabeth and Matt across the aisle from Rosemary and Gunter. Elizabeth was the widowed mother of two daughters, and she oozed sugary niceness, but if Roberta attacked her, she would glare and hiss back at her. She was short and stout with black hair, dark brown eyes and an always-present smile. She and Matt usually talked quietly between themselves.

Matt sat in the seat immediately in front of Roberta. He was married to Roberta's cousin, and his marriage was in trouble. Roberta talked about it in public with no regard for his feelings. Madeline had overheard that Matt owed Roberta a considerable sum of money that he had borrowed to get out of a financial problem. He rarely spoke, and he constantly had a sad expression on his plain face. His suit and shirt were always wrinkled, his tie loosened and hanging at an angle. According to Moira, he was a sales rep for a copier company. Madeline could not imagine him selling anything to anybody with his hangdog demeanor.

Rosemary was quite beautiful with symmetrical features and an unblemished complexion. A tall and slender blonde who always looked perfectly put together. This is a hard thing to achieve on a consistent basis at four in the morning, and Madeline was constantly amazed at her flawless hair, makeup and clothing. Some of the mystery was explained when Madeline found out she was a former model and worked for a fashion designer. According to Moira, she had never been married and flitted from man to man. She spent the majority of her bus time in deep sleep, probably to avoid the rest of her fellow passengers.

Rosemary's seat partner was a peculiar man named Gunter. Nobody knew anything about him, including his last name. A solidly built older man with iron-gray hair, he sat ramrod straight, never spoke and never seemed aware of anything going on around him. Most of the time he sat with is eyes closed as if lost in meditation. In the second row of the clique, Fern and Roberta sat across the aisle from Alice and Brian. Roberta's venomous tongue was truly a weapon. No one would cross her. Like a vicious lioness, she pounced and never apologized. She was clearly the queen of this jungle.

At first, Madeline could not understand why the other riders put up with her. Why not just ostracize her and pay no attention to her? She finally concluded everybody was exhausted and it just wasn't worth the additional effort. In the close confines of the bus there was no place to push her that would make much difference. Her voice was loud and gravelly, and could be heard clearly throughout the bus.

The one exception was Fern. Fern was her only friend, despite the fact that Roberta constantly criticized her and ordered her around like a nagging, domineering mother. She was always dressed provocatively, her curvy figure draped in some revealing outfit or clingy fabric. She had limp long blondish hair and heavily applied makeup. Her large brown eyes and cute little pointed nose, together with her blank expression, reminded Madeline of a Barbie doll. Single yet desperate to find her Prince Charming, she looked for love in all the wrong places, according to Roberta. No one could understand why Fern put up with it.

Brian was very sweet tempered. His peaceful manner was a clear contrast to Roberta's animosity toward the world. He was of average height and build with longish blond hair stuffed under an ever-present dark green baseball cap. He never raised his voice and seemed a bit lost. He loved animals and had a number of shelter dogs he had adopted. He worked for the city parks department as a groundkeeper.

Due to his placid nature, Brian ended up stuck with Alice as a seat partner. Alice was plain and prissy; in fact, she was the homeliest woman Madeline had ever seen. Hamster-brown hair cut into a bowl shape, a bad complexion, small gray eyes, a receding chin and crooked yellow teeth. She always dressed in dowdy clothes in dismal colors and sat wringing her hands, with both feet flat on the floor. If she chose to speak, Roberta would either sneer at her comment or attack her. Alice would then appear to collapse under the weight of her nasty comment with a lowered head and few sighs.

The final row of the regulars included Tony and Jake, directly behind Roberta and across from Moira and Stephen. Tony was movie-star handsome. He was tall, slim and muscular, with black hair, an olive complexion and green eyes set in a heavy-lidded, sultry gaze. His hair was casually tousled, which together with his well-manicured short stubble, gave Madeline the impression he spent a great deal of time in front of his mirror. He dressed impeccably, as if he were on the cover of a men's fashion magazine.

From what Madeline could glean from Roberta's comments, Tony was from a poor family, but due to his good looks, he had managed to marry the prettiest and wealthiest girl in town. His father-in-law was the local judge, and his mother-in-law a well-respected pediatric dentist. The former had asked a favor of an old friend and secured him a job in middle management with a real-estate management company in Manhattan. Tony was very vocal about how much he hated his job. He flirted with all the women on the bus and seemed to give Fern special attention, which irritated Roberta. Roberta made snippy comments about Tony's wife controlling the couples' purse strings and giving him a weekly allowance.

Jake worked as a union carpenter on various projects in and around Manhattan. He spoke loudly, almost shouting, so Madeline assumed he had lost some hearing because of his construction work. He was a nice-enough-looking guy, on the short side but well-built. His blond hair was cut short; he had blue eyes, a slightly off-center nose and a neatly trimmed full beard. From what she could gather, he lived alone but had a large family of siblings and cousins who lived near him and comprised his social circle, but he was not romantically attached at the moment. Apparently, he was Roberta's neighbor, and she had harassed him consistently over a variety of issues. She also made comments suggesting he was gay.

Madeline sat with Moira when her seat companion, Stephen, was not on the bus, and from her she learned a great deal about everybody. Moira was the only clique member who actually spoke to her. Madeline figured this was because she was new and politely listened to all her stories and gossip.

When Moira was not talking about other people, she was talking about herself and *my Joey*. Joey seemed to be at her beck and call and was the perfect husband, at least for Moira. She worked as the personal assistant to a trust-fund baby who managed a large and varied portfolio of investments herself. If Stephen was on the bus, Madeline sat just in front of the clique's seats, nearer to the front of the bus where *the normal people*, as she thought of them, sat.

Stephen, according to Moira, was a major mover and shaker in hedge funds and made bundles of money. Madeline mentioned to him that she worked for an investment firm and asked him where he worked, but he dodged her question, pretending not to have heard her. Madeline thought he resembled a weasel. His eyes darted around and were narrow and beady. He would never look you in the eye when he spoke to you. In his late forties, he carried extra weight around his middle, his light brown hair was thinning, and he was trying unsuccessfully to camouflage the bare spots. His manner, including his speech, was pompous, and he enjoyed telling every-body how successful he was. Madeline wondered why he was riding the bus to work if he was so successful.

CHAPTER 5

When she had moved to Cross Keys, Madeline understood there would be trade-offs. Social and cultural events she'd taken for granted when she'd lived in Manhattan were impossible now. Because she did not want to drive the Cadillac into the city, there was no practical way to get home in the evenings, so she was limited to her life in town. She began to realize she had to make the best of this situation, since her move back to Manhattan was, apparently, not happening anytime soon. The divorce was taking much longer than she had thought it would.

It was now obvious she was not going to find any friends on the bus, and opportunities to meet other people were limited by her commuting schedule. She had not even had any success meeting her neighbors. She would wave and exchange a brief greeting, but they were either elderly or couples with young children: none of them seemed eager to get to know the single woman in the big house.

Happily, new neighbors moved in next door to her, and they arrived at her door one Saturday afternoon to introduce themselves with cake and champagne. They became instant friends. Harry Wagner and Jeff Johnstone were a gay couple who had moved from the city seven years previously, leaving behind lucrative but stressful careers. Now Jeff worked in real estate, and Harry was the assistant manager at the local bank. They said they had never been happier and did not regret leaving the city at all.

Both men were attractive but completely different. Harry was tall and thin with sandy blond hair cut in a casually tousled style, while Jeff was short and plump with unruly black curly hair. Harry had dimples and bright blue eyes set in regular features, while Jeff had piercing dark eyes, a prominent Roman nose and an ever-present five-o'clock shadow. They enjoyed eating, drinking and laughing, which was exactly what Madeline needed. Since Jeff loved to cook, he made dinner, and they related all the gossip they knew from Cross Keys, and she would regale them with gossip from the bus. She saw them about every other Friday or Saturday, when they would happily drink, talk and play Rummikub until late.

As the weather grew warmer, she began to hike on weekend afternoons, walking along the river or climbing to a ridge that presented a bird's-eye view of the town and river. After living in a city for seventeen years, the beauty and wildness of the area amazed her. With almost forty percent of the county's acreage protected by either state or federal decree, the natural beauty and wildlife of the area remained largely undisturbed. There were hidden waterfalls to be discovered in the forest, along with vibrant birds and small animals rustling in the underbrush. Occasionally she would meet other hikers, but rarely, and once she saw a mother black bear in the distance with her three adorable cubs.

When it warmed up enough to sleep with her window cracked open on a regular basis, she fell in love with the peepers. The tiny tree frogs, with very big voices, sang for mates with a constant, happy sound that lulled her to sleep.

But Madeline wished she had a friend—or even a dog or a cat would be nice. Doing everything alone and coming home to an empty house was getting old fast.

CHAPTER 6

Billy sighed heavily as he dropped into his worn desk chair. He replaced the front left wheel, which always fell off, and adjusted his lumbar-support cushion, a gift his last girlfriend had given him when she'd left him. It was a needlepoint pillow reading *Of all the things I've lost, I miss my mind the most.* Finally settled at his desk, he pondered the Grickly murder as he watched his pencil roll to the edge of the desk. Each time it was ready to fall off, he saved it and set it down to roll again. He had attempted to level the desk, but it required so many books under both front legs that his chair was too low and its height could not be adjusted. It didn't help that the old and not well-maintained building that housed the police station was slowly sinking on one side. After finally accepting the tilted desk as a permanent condition, he'd decided to think of his pencil-rolling as a form of meditation. It did, in fact, help him concentrate.

Grickly's body was found in Cross Keys, but he had lived in Port Potter. His business had spanned the river to include all the neighboring towns. The police had done all the initial legwork, including canvassing the neighborhood around the Tickity for witnesses, and notifying and interviewing Grickly's next of kin, but had not discovered anything helpful. So now it was time for Billy to dig deeper into Grickly's life and criminal activities. He put in a call to Al DoLuca, chief of the Port Potter police. He had all the background on Grickly and willingly agreed to share what information he had.

Billy headed for Port Potter just ten miles north across the Delaware. It had been a boomtown around the turn of the twentieth century, when canals were an important part of the transportation process. Once the canals were replaced by trains and then interstate highways and trucks, it had slowly gone downhill as many businesses left, and with them, the hardworking people they employed. During the last thirty years, it had become a town populated by transients. The once-bustling downtown with large and beautiful homes and attractive stores became block after block of liquor stores, pawnshops and thrift stores sprinkled among abandoned buildings. The police station was one of the few new buildings in town, as crime seemed to be the only growth industry there these days. It was a squat rectangular box sandwiched between two old three-story office buildings. One housed a law office, and the other offered bail bonds and a travel agency.

Chief DoLuca greeted Billy with a warm handshake and ushered him into his office. He motioned for Billy to sit. "I cannot tell you how happy we are that, if Bart had to die under mysterious circumstances, he did it on your turf."

Billy nodded and grinned. "Well, I wondered if you guys had planted the body to avoid the hassle."

Al shook his head and smiled. "Wish I was that clever. So, got any leads?"

"No. Looks like he was attacked from behind. Strangled with a piece of rope that you can buy just about anywhere. No fingerprints, DNA, security camera footage or even tire tracks or footprints for that matter. And no witnesses so far."

Al nodded sympathetically. "God knows he had loads of people who would have loved to see him gone. Well, you'll want to talk to his live-in, Joelle Babcock, and if you are lucky, she might be coherent. The kind of girl you can take home to Mom, as long as Mom likes part-time prostitutes and certified junkies."

He pushed a thick file folder across his desk toward Billy. "That folder contains most of the information I have on Bart Grickly, except for the juvenile records, of course. You can borrow it for a while. Some of it is in the computer files, but some isn't."

"Thanks. Can you give me the Reader's Digest version?"

Al smiled and leaned back in his comfortable chair. "Sure. Bart was my special project for a lot of years, as you know. He was born here and grew up in Port and in Lyon. His father was in prison off and on until he finally got life for an armed robbery and murder. He hit a convenience store in Madison and shot the teenage clerk through the neck. He claimed it was by accident, but the jury did not find his story credible. Bart's mother was, well, the kind of woman who would marry an armed robber and murderer and never leave him no matter how much he abused her and their children.

"There were three kids: Betty, Bart and Joe. Bart was the middle one and the smart one, and he was fast, strong and athletic. He was Dad's pride and joy. Betty, the oldest, got pregnant during her freshman year in high school. It turned out old man Grickly was the father. Betty lost the baby just before Dad went to jail, and the family moved to Lyon. I found this out from my sister-in-law, who was the school counselor back then. Things only got worse, of course. Betty became the class whore and committed suicide at nineteen. Joe had some kind of mental malfunction. He still lives with Mom in their mobile home in Lyon. Bart became a big deal on the Cross Keys High School football team as a running back. Road Runner they called him. You remember that?"

Billy nodded. "Yeah, they were state champions that year. Best team we ever had."

"There was talk that he could make it to college on a scholarship and maybe turn pro, but that was always a sky-high dream. What chance did he have? His father was a convicted felon, and his mother became a drunk after Betty's suicide. She worked on and off at the Walmart to make ends meet. Maybe turned a trick from time to time. Bart just drifted, no direction, ran with a bad crowd. Got into crime. The rest is in the file. We never could catch him in anything important enough to get him off the street for any length of time."

"Any chance I can search his home? Do you think his girlfriend will let me look around?"

Al shook his head. "She may be a junkie, but she is too savvy about her rights for that. It would be better to get a warrant. I'll get Judge Hainsworth to issue a one. Won't take but an hour or so."

"Thanks. I can study the file while I wait. Got any coffee?"

"Well, we call it coffee but it has also been called less respectable names," Al said as he led him into a break room and pointed to the coffee machine.

* * *

Grickly's home turned out to be a very run-down Victorian house right in downtown Port Potter. Billy had to knock on the door several times, as the doorbell was not working.

"Who are you, and what the hell do you want?" a woman's weary voice shouted from behind the door.

"I'm Police Chief West from Cross Keys. I'm here concerning Bart Grickly's death," Billy yelled through the door.

An extremely thin young woman with a pasty-white face surrounded by long, greasy brown hair opened the door slightly. She wore ripped jeans, a stained, faded T-shirt and no shoes.

"Yeah. The police were here already. What do you want now?"

"I need to ask you a few questions. Can I come in?"

Joelle glared at Billy. "Not unless you have a warrant."

Billy stared back at her and grinned. "Got it right here," he said as he took the paper from his pocket. Joelle looked it over quickly, then begrudgingly opened the door to let him in. The large room she led them to was full of empty fast-food containers, newspapers and other trash. It had once been a fine great room with custom wood paneling and a high ceiling surrounded with crown molding. But now the burgundy flocked wallpaper was peeling and the once-white ceiling had large brown stains. A big plasma TV tuned to a court TV show was blasting at one end of the room, and a desk piled high with paper stood at the opposite end. In between, there was a badly worn and soiled sofa and a newer-looking leather recliner.

"Sit, if you dare," Joelle waved in the direction of the sofa as she sat in the recliner.

"Thanks, but I like to stand," said Billy, as he looked around the room. "I'm sorry about your loss, Mrs. Grickly."

Joelle smirked and nodded. She lit a cigarette and took a drag. "Thanks for your heartfelt sympathy, Chief. By the way, we wasn't man and wife. Bart never got around to the on-one-knee proposal with the diamond ring."

"What can you tell me about his last day?"

She shrugged her thin shoulders and looked at Billy with large, dark, lifeless eyes. "Not much to tell. Bart had some bets to pay off and some money to collect. He did most of it early. But he still needed to find a couple of people, so we went to the Tickity in Cross Keys that night."

"So, you went with him?"

"Yeah, but just to the bar. His collection runs were boring as shit. He liked to socialize with the clients. He could talk about nothing for hours with the biggest losers." She glared at Billy. "In case you think I know shit. I paid no attention to his business. I know nothing about it."

"What time did you go to the bar?"

"It was early. I guess about nine or nine thirty." She tamped the cigarette in the overflowing ashtray and lit another one.

"What time did you leave?"

"Well, that old bitch bartender threw us out 'cause she wanted to close and get her sorry old bones to bed, I guess." She shrugged. "Maybe around eleven."

"Where did you and Bart go then?"

Joelle looked puzzled as she took a drag from her cigarette. "I guess we came home."

"You guess?"

"Well, I was high, man. I blacked out. When I woke up, I was in bed."

"So, you don't know anything else about that night or what Bart did?"

Joelle smirked. "That's right. I have no idea what happened."

"Did he ever talk about any of his...clients?"

"Yeah, but he didn't make much sense."

"What do you mean?" Billy snapped at her.

Joelle sat up straighter. "Well, he had nicknames for everything and everybody. I gave up listening." She took a deep drag. "He called me Stick," she said in a soft whisper.

Billy looked around the room for a minute. "Did he mention anything about one of them being a problem? Any threats?"

Joelle blew smoke rings toward the ceiling as she thought. "No," she finally said.

"How did he keep track of his business? Did he have a computer or laptop?"

Joelle looked annoyed. "Oh, man. Bart hated computers and cell phones. He only used one 'cause he had to for business, and it was a flip phone. No texting or email for him. He thought the government could track him, listen in and read everything, you know. He used the computers at the library to get the latest betting odds. But he kept everything in his head, except for the book."

"What book?" Billy said sternly as he was beginning to lose hope. "Yeah, he had this leather book. If anybody touched it, he had a shit fit."

"Do you know where this book is?"

"Might be in the desk." Joelle waved her cigarette in the general direction of the desk. "Knock yourself out. You got the warrant."

Billy walked over to the desk and looked down at the top, overflowing with various old newspapers all turned to the sports pages.

He opened the center drawer and found a collection of pencils, pens, paper clips and other office supplies. The left-hand top drawer was full of what appeared to be mail. The middle drawer was entirely empty except for a leather journal. Billy held it up. "Is this it?"

She nodded, lighting another cigarette.

Billy opened it up and looked at a list of names such as Home Wrecker, Pothead, Henpecked and Bitch. Across from each name was a number, which he assumed was a dollar amount, a date and then a team name. Thumbing through to the back of the book, he found a list of teams, dates and what he assumed were the spreads. Tucked into the back between the leather cover and the endpaper was a photo of Bart in his football uniform looking handsome and arrogant. He was standing surrounded by other members of the team, with the caption *Road Runner and the Coyotes* written in ink across the bottom.

Along with the photo was a lined yellow sheet of paper. Billy pulled it out and opened it. It contained a list of *Specials*, with nicknames, dates and dollar amounts, and some had additional numbers with a letter next to them. The dollar amounts on this list were much larger than the betting amounts. There were six names at the top of the Specials list: Fatso, Dumbo, Romeo, Ditsy, Cinderfella and Pathetic. Additional names were listed below, with some having been crossed out or having question marks next to them. "You don't know who any of these people might be?" Billy read from the book. "Shorty, Stinky, Crazy, Henpecked, Bitch..."

Joelle laughed. "*Bitch*. Man he hit it on the head with that one."

"Did you know her?"

"Yeah, ugly broad from Keys. She came by a lot. Way too much. Usually barged right in without even asking. Acted like she owned the place. Really pissed us off. One time, a while ago, she pushed right past me and walked in on Bart. He was meeting with one of his special clients, and that really pissed him off. She acted like it was a family reunion since she knew the guy. She came by the day after Bart died. Said he owed her money."

Joelle sighed in exasperation. "I told her I didn't know where his money was. She glared at me like she was gonna hit me. I told her to back off and get the hell out."

"Well, what did she look like?"

"She's short and mean looking. Thin, frizzy brown hair, big glasses, loud mouth..."

"What was her name?" Billy asked, even though he had a good idea who this was about.

"I told you. I don't know the names. He just called her Bitch."

"Could it be Roberta Carlson?"

Joelle just shrugged.

Billy handed her his card. "If you remember anything, give me a call. I'll take the book for now. I'll show myself out."

Joelle lit another cigarette as she watched him leave.

Even though it was his first lead, he didn't relish the thought of interviewing Roberta Carlson. But he had to admit Grickly had nailed her with the nickname.

CHAPTER 7

The Tick-Tock Lounge, or the Tickity as the locals called it, was located on the east side of High Street on the north edge of town. A few blocks past it, High Street expanded into a three-lane road leading to Walmart, strip malls, Lyon and Port Potter.

The bar was originally opened in 1954, and at that time it was considered to be the hippest spot in all of northeastern Pennsylvania. Now it was just dilapidated and shabby, its original fifties decorative motifs worn out. The giant mahogany bar was shaped like a boomerang and was deeply scarred from years of use. Behind the bar hung a large clock; its neon-blue face had *Tick-Tock* written in yellow-neon cursive script across it. The time was always wrong. On either side of the clock, metal sconces shaped like rocket ships allowed pinpricks of light to shine through the metal. A suspended ceiling shaped like an artist's palette hung low over the bar area. The tile floor was set in a wave pattern of alternating white and black. The tables and chairs were unremarkably modern, adding nothing to the decor, but the barstools had wooden seats shaped like boomerangs.

Agatha Clarkson was the current proprietor. Tall and slender with thick white hair cut to shoulder length in layers and bangs. Subtle makeup defined and enhanced her sparkling blue eyes. Her skin was china-doll white and unblemished, with fine lines all over her face that deepened around her eyes and mouth. She always wore deep red lipstick. She and her late husband had owned the bar together. After he died, she had taken over while raising her two teenage boys. She was tough as nails, but she had a soft spot for both Billy and Tom.

"Hi, Agatha," Billy said as he sat down at the bar. Billy loved to look at Agatha. In his opinion, she was the classiest woman in town.

"Hi, Billy." She smiled at him. "I was wondering when you were going to show up. I know you've talked to my employees and the entire neighborhood. Your usual?"

Billy nodded, and she put a Coke in front of him. "I always save the best for last." Billy gave her his most charming smile. "So, Bart spent his last night alive in your bar."

"Yes, he was here all right, him and that Joelle. He just made my skin crawl every time he came in."

Billy nodded. "What time did Grickly get here, and how long did he stay?"

Agatha looked thoughtful for a moment. "Oh, I think that he came in around nine thirty and didn't leave until close to closing, around eleven thirty. Oh, and before you ask, I was home and asleep by one. But my only witness is Ginger, my cat."

"Noted. Did Bart talk to anybody in particular?"

Agatha thought another minute. "Yeah, he was here to do business. He talked to a few people. Some money changed hands. Nobody I knew. I hated it when he used my bar as his office." Agatha shrugged. "I told him so, but he just laughed at me. Said it was a free country."

"Any locals?"

"As far as my regular customers go, Roberta was here with Fern. At one point Roberta started screeching at Bart about money. I think. I didn't catch the entire conversation. It got loud, so I told them to take it outside. They were right in front of the window. She was giving Bart hell, from the look of it. They were only out there, oh, maybe five minutes. Then she stormed back in, grabbed Fern and left."

"Anybody else here that night you remember?"

"Tony Fowler was here with some of his old buddies. One is fat with a lot of hair, and the other has a ridiculous man bun. Bart knew them too."

Billy nodded. "Thank you for your help, Agatha. If you think of anything else..."

"I will be sure to give you a call."

"Oh, congrats on becoming a grandmother!" Billy said as he stood up to leave.

"Oh, thanks, Billy. But I have to say that it makes me feel old." Agatha could not repress her smile. "He's sweet as can be. And good-looking too. Looks just like his grandmother."

"He's a lucky kid. And you certainly don't look any older to me."

Agatha laughed. "You better be careful. One day your flirting is going to get you in trouble."

"It already has." Billy waved as he walked out of the door.

CHAPTER 8

Roberta and Samantha Carlson shared a house in the prestigious private community of Whispering Pines. It was set in a beautiful, forested area with a large spring-fed lake. The houses were set on a minimum of an acre so, unlike other lake communities, the houses were not on top of each other. The sisters' home was a modern log cabin neatly tucked away behind tall pine trees, with a good view of the lake and easy access to it. They had a neat lawn with a large andromeda in flower and other decorative plantings beginning to bud.

Billy rang the doorbell and waited. He had called ahead, so he knew Roberta was home. After about five minutes the door finally opened.

"Hello, Roberta. I hate to disturb you ladies..."

"But you will anyway." Roberta scowled at him. "Let's get this over with." She abruptly turned her back on him as she walked back into the house.

Billy gently closed the door behind him and followed her. The interior of the house was sparkling clean and neat, decorated in an early American or colonial style, complete with a spinning wheel sitting next to the fireplace, a Pennsylvania blanket chest under the window and comfortable-looking sofa and chairs upholstered in a red-checked homespun fabric. Plaster figurines, needlepoint pillows and family photos filled every available surface and shelf. Decorative plates depicting Labrador retrievers, miscellaneous puppies at play, bunnies and baby fur seals adorned the log walls.

He followed Roberta into the large kitchen to find Fern and Samantha sitting at the kitchen table.

"Hi, Chief," they said in greeting.

"Please sit down," said Roberta's sister. "Can I get you some coffee and cake?"

"Really, Sam? He's here to question me about Bart Grickly's murder, and you offer him coffee and cake?"

"No thank you, Samantha," Billy said calmly as he remained standing.

Roberta collapsed into a kitchen table chair and sighed heavily. "I didn't kill Bart. And you're an idiot if you think that I did."

"Well, maybe so, but you did speak to Bart at the Tickity on the night he was murdered. I've been informed the conversation got heated. Why?"

"Well, I have to say that I am surprised that you would know that, Billy. I guess you have been working after all." She scowled up at him through her thick glasses. "I had won five hundred on the Knicks and I was feeling lucky, so I let it ride on the next game."

"It was *our* money," Samantha interrupted. "Letting it ride was your idea."

"Yeah, yeah. As you can see, Pain in the Ass here wanted her half of the winnings. She didn't want to let it ride on the next game. So, I asked for the money, and he blew me off. Said the bet was already placed and that was that. So, naturally, I wasn't going to take that shit so I argued with him, and then he said he didn't have the cash on him, but he had some more to collect and might have it later. I didn't like to leave things hanging with him. He wasn't the most upstanding citizen, you know. So, I figured I'd go back later. The Tickity was closed down for the night when I passed by; in fact, the entire town was closed from what I could see. So, I went to his home in Port. The house was dark, and nobody answered my knocking and yelling. So, I checked all the dives in Port and Lyon that were still open, but no luck. So, I came home. End of a sad story. I will never get the money now."

"You still owe me my part, you know," Samantha huffed.

"Yeah, yeah."

"You also showed up at his house the morning after he died."

"Robbie!" Samantha and Fern said in unison.

"Will you two settle down!" Roberta looked exasperated. "Do I have to spoon-feed you everything, West? When I found out he was dead, I figured I better get my...*our* money before that druggie girlfriend of his did. I gave her a rough time, but it was obvious that she knew nothing."

"How did you know he was dead?" Billy asked.

"I heard it at the deli when I went to get my breakfast bagel. I go every Saturday morning. You can check with that tubby woman who works there. She told me. I headed right for Port Potter."

"So, all this running around was just because you wanted Samantha's money?"

"Exactly what part of what I said did you not understand? Yes. And I still want *all* my money." She sat back in her chair with her arms crossed and her mouth tightly shut into a firm line.

"Did you know any of the other people in the Tickity that night?"

"Sure. Tony Fowler was there."

"Other than Tony, did you know anybody?"

"No. It was just scum from Port Potter and some stupid tourist couples. Right, Fern?"

"Yes. We didn't know anybody but Tony and Bart," Fern confirmed.

"Did either of you two see Bart arguing with anybody that night?"

"Not that I recall," Roberta said. Fern shook her head.

"What time did you two leave the bar?"

"It was about ten thirty, 'cause Fern wanted to be home to watch one of her stupid TV romance movies."

"When did you go back out to look for him?"

"I don't remember. I don't punch a time clock, you know. Midnight or a little after, I guess. I already told you I never found him."

"Joelle said you came by the house on a regular basis."

"How would she know? She's only conscious once a month. Yeah, I did go by to collect my winnings. I didn't trust Bart." She glared at Billy. "I will spell it out for you, since you can't seem to figure it out. I don't know who killed him. That is your job to find out, so I suggest you leave us alone and go find the killer."

Billy silently counted to ten while he flipped his notebook closed. "Thank you for your time, ladies. I will see myself out," he said with a smile.

Billy completed his notes in his car. "Yep, *Bitch* is definitely Roberta," he muttered to himself.

* * *

Billy sat at The Opossum bar drinking coffee and impatiently staring at the door.

"Where have you been?" Billy snapped at Tom as he entered.

"Sorry, Billy! Have you been drinking too much coffee again? You know too much caffeine makes you snippy like an old man. Or can I assume the investigation is not going smoothly?"

Billy looked down at his cup.

"That good, huh?"

"That's sort of why I'm here. You got a minute?"

"Sure. Let's head up to my office."

They climbed the creaking, worn steps, and Tom unlocked the door and switched on the light. His small office was on the cramped second floor of the building. *Second floor* was a generous description as it was little more than a low-ceiling attic with most of the open space serving as storage. The small office was the only actual room and was located at the front of the building where the roof peaked, making the ceiling higher. It had a small window overlooking the alley entrance.

The previous owner had purchased the office furniture from a retiring insurance salesman in the 1950s. A large, sturdy oak desk stood in front of the window. It had a gooseneck lamp on the left-hand side and a metal letter tray on the right side. A few papers were piled next to a closed laptop on the green leather desk blotter. The four-drawer oak filing cabinet stood against the wall opposite the desk. Two wooden chairs sat in front of the desk, and a third with wheels behind. A well-worn burgundy leather loveseat was against one wall, with a bronze floor lamp with an alabaster-white shade next to it. The floor space in front of the loveseat was covered with a traditionally designed oriental area rug in terracotta and navy blue. Above the small sofa hung a large detailed map of Cross Keys and the surrounding area.

"So, what's up?" Tom said as he sat down behind the desk.

Billy plopped into one of the guest chairs. "Well, I've done all the legwork. No witnesses. Not a shred of helpful evidence. Except this." Billy pushed the leather-bound notebook over to him. "It's Grickly's ledger."

Tom opened the book and began to study each page. "Who are these people? *Stinky, Sexy, Sneezy, Pathetic?*"

"That's the problem. I know for sure who a dozen of his regular customers were, but who corresponds to which name is anybody's guess. And look in the back."

Tom flipped to the back of the book and picked up the photo of the high-school hero Bart and friends. He fished out the yellow piece of paper and looked at the list of Specials then at Billy. "Any idea what *Specials* means?"

Billy shrugged. "Maybe blackmail."

"Do the so-called Special names appear on the betting list also? If so, you need to find the gambler with the biggest secret."

"Yeah, two do. Romeo and Ditsy. So, how do I find out the secret? And what if the dozen people I know of aren't the ones on the list?"

"You have no idea about who's who?"

"I know one. *Bitch* is..."

"Roberta!" Tom whooped, and Billy nodded.

"Well, maybe they are all that obvious once you think about it."

"Maybe."

"Yes, it looks as though *Bitch* had done well on the Knicks, according to Bart's book. And it appears she let her money ride on the next game."

"Yes, Roberta mentioned that. She's mad she can't get her money."

"I have no problem believing that."

"Yeah. She's not on the Specials list."

"Well, that's no surprise. I doubt anybody would have the nerve to blackmail her, even a guy like Grickly. No amount of money could pay for that aggravation."

"I talked to her about his last night. They were at the Tickity at the same time."

"Did she have anything useful to offer?"

"No."

Tom picked up the photo and studied it. "Why'd he keep the photo, I wonder? Grickly didn't seem like the sentimental type."

Billy shrugged. "Better days? What might have been? Apparently, he had dreams of going pro back then."

"So, if this is a list of people Bart was blackmailing, I would think they are the most likely to have wanted him dead." He tapped the photo against the book. "Let me borrow this for a couple of days. I need to think about it."

"Thanks. I was hoping you'd volunteer. But naturally I can't let you have it, so I made a copy for you." He grinned as he handed Tom a manila envelope.

"How did Bart die?"

"He was strangled from behind with a piece of common rope."

"Even with a surprise attack, it would take strength. Bart was—what?—about six feet? So, a short, weak person couldn't have done it."

Billy nodded. "Let's Roberta off, I guess."

"Unless she hired someone to..."

"Good point. Let me know what you come up with. It's all just between us as usual, right?"

"Absolutely."

CHAPTER 9

Tom walked into the diner with a broad smile on his handsome face.

"Good morning, Tom." May welcomed him with a big smile.

"Good morning, May! How are you this fine day?"

"My, we are cheery today, aren't we?" she said while giving him a flirty glance.

Tom sat on the first stool on the right-end of the counter and looked down High Street as he sipped his coffee. He looked pensive. "Must be the warm breeze and smell of spring."

"You want waffles or pancakes today?"

Tom looked thoughtful. "French toast, I think. I feel like a change."

May giggled and said, "Well, if that is the biggest change you can think of, you need to get out more."

Tom smiled and watched as a steady line of people streamed in and out of Bolter's, the newspaper, magazine and candy store on the corner of High Street across from the library.

Billy sat down on the stool next to Tom.

"Good morning, Billy," Tom and May said in unison.

"It's cherry today," May said as she indicated the pie with a nod of her head.

"I didn't even ask. Yet." Billy looked thoughtful. "Okay, I will try a nice big piece," he said with a broad smile.

Tom laughed and shook his head. "I do not understand why you don't weigh five hundred pounds with the amount of pie you eat. It's not as if you exercise. You ride around in a car most of the day and sit in a broken desk chair the rest of the time."

"Hey, who says I don't exercise?" Billy looked hurt and then smiled broadly. "I'm just lucky, I guess. Some of us are just excellent physical specimens, Tom. You're just going to have to get over it. Right, May?"

"No comment," May said laughing as she gave him his pie and coffee.

Billy took a huge bite. "Good pie, May." He looked over at Tom. "Any progress with, you know, the thing I gave you?"

"Nothing yet. But I do have some news. Remember my old partner, Ralph—" Tom started.

"The PI you used to work with?"

"Yes. Well, he is retiring, closing up shop, clearing out his office and apartment in Manhattan. He's going to move to North Carolina near his daughter and grandchildren. He asked me if I was interested in taking over the business."

Billy looked startled and stopped eating his pie. "You said no, I hope?"

"Yes. He knew I would, but he thought he would give me one last chance before he sells it. He's been reasonably successful over the years. But he asked if I would help him pack up. So, I told him I would."

"You going to stay in the city?"

"No. I figure I will take the bus on a daily basis. I may not need to go in every day and, if I do, it should just be for a few weeks."

"Wouldn't you rather drive?"

"I thought about it, but it takes almost the same amount of time, and it's more expensive with the tolls and parking on top of gas. At least I can nap and read on the bus."

Billy nodded in understanding as he tucked into his pie again. "Who's going to take care of The Opossum while you're away?"

Tom laughed. "I'm not going across the country. I'll be back every evening, and I'll probably be here most weekends. Adam and Debby can handle the day-to-day."

"When is this adventure going to start?"

"Probably next week. Ralph has some loose ends to tie up on a couple of jobs. But I can start packing up the old files."

Tom turned to see Roberta and Fern walking up to the counter.

"Well, if it isn't the Cross Keys dynamic duo." Roberta's piercing voice filled the diner. "Fighting crime the old fashion way, West? Watching for traffic offenses out the window while sitting on your pudgy ass eating pie? Firemark is probably sober at this hour, so maybe he can help you."

"Nice to see you too, Roberta," Tom said.

"We'll be over at our usual booth," she said to May. "Bring us our coffee when you're done serving these losers." She turned sharply and walked away with Fern in tow.

"Just think. You'll get to commute within the close confines of a bus with those two," Billy whispered to Tom.

"Good point. Maybe I should think more seriously about driving."

CHAPTER 10

Madeline struggled to board the bus. She was carrying several shopping bags plus her purse and her bus tote for all the things that she had to carry to and from work: a blow-up travel pillow, a small blanket, an umbrella, snacks, water and her iPad. She was riding the 5:37, the second afternoon bus, rather than her usual 4:32 and did not recognize any of the other passengers. She put her bags in the overhead compartment and sighed heavily as she settled into a window seat and closed her eyes.

"Do you mind if I sit here?" Madeline looked up to see Tom looking at her. She suddenly felt awake.

"Oh, please sit down! I thought I saw you sitting in the first row this morning, but I couldn't catch you after we all got off."

"I was the last one on. I almost missed the bus this morning."

"What are you doing on the bus?"

"Commuting for a short while. I'm helping an old friend close down his business and move. I worked with him years ago."

"That's nice of you. What kind of business?"

"He's a private investigator."

"So, you were a private investigator? That sounds interesting. Lots of mystery, murders and intrigue, with damsels in distress and conspiracies to uncover."

Tom laughed. "If only it were that interesting. It was really very mundane and even depressing. A lot of divorce cases, some insurance fraud, background checks and the occasional missing person. Very few endangered damsels or conspiracies. You would be amazed at the number of people who are not what they appear or pretend to be. It can destroy your faith in humanity, providing you had any to start with. Ralph—that's my friend—he hired me when I was at a really low point. He took a chance on me. I had no experience investigating. He had to train me from scratch. Now he's a good friend."

"Did you buy the bar after you stopped being a PI?"

Tom nodded. "Yes. It came on the market just after my father died. I inherited enough to buy it. Going through family papers after his death, I found out that my great-grandfather had been a part owner years ago. It seemed like the perfect opportunity."

"So, you mentioned your great-grandfather lived in Cross Keys. Were you born here?"

"Yes. I grew up there. My father was the town doctor, when doctors still made house calls, treated every ailment without a specialist and were considered pillars of the community. My mother was the classic stay-at-home mom, with women's clubs and church committees to keep her busy. I am essentially an only child. My older brother, Danny, died of leukemia at the age of ten. He was only a year and three months older than me. At that time, cancer of any kind was a death sentence. We grieved as a family. My father said he had seen too many people bottle up their grief and never get over it. We had many conversations about life and death. Eventually life went on."

Madeline was silent for a few minutes as she stared out the bus window. "It must have been a nice place to grow up," she finally said.

"Yes, it was. I did not appreciate it at the time, and I made some bad decisions as a young man."

"It seems to be human nature to not appreciate things until after we lose them," Madeline said softly.

Tom was usually reluctant to talk about himself, but he felt comfortable with Madeline. She was unpretentious, kind and fun. "Looking back, I cannot imagine what I was thinking. In school, I was the smart kid. You know, the one who didn't do any studying, just read the textbook the day before the test and aced it. My mother tried very hard to make me be a better student, but I was young and liked the easy way. The first thing I did after graduation was elope with my high-school sweetheart."

"That was a bold move."

"That is one way to look at it. Our parents were furious. We were together about six months and divorced within a year. I worked in a meat-packing plant in New Jersey to support us. It was a bitter lesson. So, that delayed my starting college. When I went to college, my bad study habits caught up with me, and I ended up dropping out after two years. My parents said they would support me through graduate school, but if I dropped out, I was on my own."

"So, I would guess that was another rude awakening."

"Oh, yes. I wasn't as smart as I thought, and I was disillusioned with true love. But I was stubborn and wanted to prove to my parents they were wrong and I could make it on my own. It was rough going. But my ability to learn quickly did come in handy. I had so many jobs I can't even remember them all. Name a job and I have probably done it."

"Short order cook," Madeline suggested.

"Yes."

"Prison guard."

"No. But I was a bounty hunter briefly."

"Bus driver."

"No. But I did drive a tractor trailer, so truck driver."

"Circus clown."

"No. But I was a roustabout. I had to help bury an elephant once."

Madeline laughed. "Okay, I get the picture."

"I didn't last more than a few weeks in many of my career choices. But I drove a truck for the longest time. I got to see a large part of the US by doing that. It was lonely, so I adopted a dog, Tug. He was great company."

"Oh! I love dogs. What kind of dog?" Madeline gushed.

"Some kind of mutt. He had a scruffy beard and floppy ears. He was really smart. Once I fell asleep at the wheel, and he barked right in my ear and woke me up."

"I had a dog when I met John, my husband. After she died, he wouldn't let me get another one. So, how did you become a private investigator?"

"I was driving the truck, and I was having a late lunch at a truck stop in Maine. The guy sitting next to me at the counter was showing the waitress a photograph and asking if she had seen the person. He later told me he literally asked every person he met. We struck up a conversation, and I found out he was a PI looking for a missing person, a young woman who had disappeared about six years before.

"At first, they had looked hard for her, but there were no leads and they gave up. Her father, who was apparently a real SOB and was the main reason she'd left, just wrote her off. When he died, the mother and grandmother really wanted to find her. They were wealthy, so they told Ralph to spend whatever he needed to. He put ads in local newspapers across the country and even hired local investigators to help him find her. This was the old days before Facebook and Google could help you locate people.

"After searching all over the country, he finally figured it was going to be just dumb luck if he found her at that point. He had a gut feeling that she was in the northeast, but that was still a large area to cover. He had done all he could, and when we met, he was about to reluctantly give up. He ended up giving me a copy of the photo. It was an old picture of her as a teenager, and he asked if I would keep my eyes open, since I was covering so much ground. Ralph and I sat talking over coffee and then switched to beers and continued to talk late into the night. We had a real connection. We talked about everything, about his life, my life and life in general. We parted friends."

"So, you found her?"

Tom nodded. "I was in upstate New York near Lake Ontario, and Tug got sick. He was dying, in fact. I went to the first vet I found, and when I carried him into the clinic, I saw her sitting at the reception desk. Turned out the vet was her husband, and she was about seven months pregnant. I called Ralph, and it was apparently a great family reunion. I still get a Christmas card from her every year with a family photo. The kids are grown now, but there are five of them and at least three dogs, two cats and a goat, cow or pig in every photo.

"Ralph was elated, kept thanking me profusely and offered to pay me, but I said no. It was in fact luck. I essentially stumbled upon her. That's when he offered me a job. He said my varied work experience would come in handy. Plus, someone with the ability to recognize a person out of context and years later than the photo was hard to come by. He was impressed I had recognized her. She had grown up and looked very different from the photo."

"How did you recognize her?"

"Her eyes. Eyes don't change much over the years."

Madeline nodded. "So, you accepted the job offer?"

"I was getting tired of driving around, living the nomadic trucker life. With Tug gone, I felt rootless and lonely. I was homesick. The job was in Manhattan, and it got me closer to home. So, I took it. I had kept in touch with my parents by phone and mail, but I only saw them when a route took me through Pennsylvania. I was happy to settle in one place again. And I did reconnect with my parents.

"It turned out to be the perfect job for me. Even my father thought so. He said I had always been good at looking at a situation and figuring out what was going on or what had happened."

"Any particular reason he thought that?" Madeline asked.

"That is another long story."

"Well, we have plenty of time."

Tom grinned. "Yes, we do. Enough about me. Are you enjoying living in the country?"

"I'm doing okay. It's just that it is all a big change from living in the city. The commute is exhausting. Some nights all I can do is get home and fall asleep. But I am doing some hiking and getting to know the area a bit on weekends. You know. Driving around and sightseeing."

"Good. Sounds like you are settling in."

They sat in silence for a few seconds. "So, I know you inherited your house from your great-aunt, and I know you are divorcing your husband, but I don't know anything else about you."

"Oh. Well. My life has not been nearly as interesting as yours. Pretty typical, I think. I was raised in the suburbs of New York in a nice house, in a nice neighborhood with excellent schools. My parents couldn't have children, so they adopted a baby boy. Then—surprise, surprise!—I came along when my mother was forty-five. I was never close to my brother. A large age difference, and I think he was jealous. He was an only child for almost twelve years. I would come to Cross Keys for summer visits with my grandmother and aunt, and he never wanted to come along.

"I went to college and met John my freshman year. He was three years ahead of me. We were both accounting majors. I think bookkeeper is one occupation you missed, right?

"We each went our own way after college. I lived the single life in the city and had a good time. I worked at two firms and finally found the one I work for now. John and I ran into each other by accident one day and reconnected and finally got married. We had a great marriage, or so I thought. We traveled a lot. Interesting and, for me, adventurous trips. We went scuba diving at an uninhabited island in the Pacific with sharks. We got there on a sailboat from Costa Rica. We stayed in a rainforest lodge in Borneo. And we enjoyed the city. We went to restaurants, art openings, the theater, and we had season tickets to Carnegie Hall concerts." Madeline was silent for a moment then she let out a big sigh. "But he found someone else. End of story. My parents died when I was in my midtwenties, one right after the other a couple of years apart. The last contact I had with my brother was at my mother's funeral. Like I said, not much of a story. No exciting twists and turns."

"Excitement is not all it is cracked up to be."

"Are you going to be on the bus every day?" Madeline asked, hoping she did not appear too excited by the prospect.

Tom nodded. "Yes, it looks like I will be commuting for a month or so."

"What about The Opossum?"

"I'll be able to show up most nights and on weekends. Plus, I am available by phone if Adam has a problem he can't handle."

"That will make for some pretty long days."

"It is not forever."

"Well, I am happy to have you aboard!"

Their conversation dwindled, and they fell silent, each thinking their own thoughts, as the rocking motion of the bus finally lulled them to sleep.

CHAPTER 11

Now that Tom was commuting, Madeline had a steady seat companion. She felt they were becoming real friends. It made a big difference to have someone to talk with or just sit in companionable silence with during the long ride home after a hard day at the office. They had taken to sitting in the last row, which was designed to seat three people. If the bus was not crowded, it gave them extra room, and Tom could sit in the open aisle seat and stretch out his legs. If the bus was full, it forced Madeline to sit almost on top of Tom. She preferred a crowded bus.

This cozy arrangement had not gone unnoticed by the clique in general or by Roberta in particular. Roberta was constantly pointing out to Madeline that Tom had a wicked past and that she was wasting her time "throwing her fat ass" at him, making it clear she was not his type. Tom just ignored her, and Madeline appeared to, but she did decide to start a serious diet and walk around more during her lunch hour.

One Friday evening, Tom boarded the bus and noticed the regulars were holding paper plates, napkins, plastic forks and glasses. "What's going on today?" Tom asked as he sat down next to Madeline.

"Apparently, it is something called the Spring Soiree," Madeline said with a slight shrug.

On an erratic and whimsical schedule, the clique of regulars on the 4:32 bus had parties featuring alcohol and food. The parties made the clique happy, but it increased the amount of noise they made, which did not endear them to the passengers who were excluded from the festivities. They tried to protest, but Roberta shouted them down. Even Martha, the evening driver, who was in command of the bus and could accept or deny any and all activities, decided that life was too short to deal with Roberta and just put up with the occasional party.

Once the bus was out of the Lincoln Tunnel, the party was officially started by Stephen when he opened one of the bottles of red wine that he habitually contributed to the events. He ceremoniously presented the first bottle for the group's approval. They all nodded knowingly, and then he began to pour a small glass for each person except Jake, who didn't like wine, so he brought his own beer, and Alice who never drank anything stronger than water.

Everyone contributed by bringing food or paper goods. The theme today was Mexican because Roberta insisted upon it, and so the food included bean dip and Fritos, salsa and guacamole with tortilla chips, gazpacho, cheesy nachos and, for those not in favor of

Mexican food, cheese with crackers and fresh vegetable strips with a yogurt dip. The sweets included Devil Dogs and M&M's.

Stephen held his glass high as he said, "May we all win the lottery and never have to ride this terrible bus again!" Enthusiastic agreement came from the group.

"Pour me some more, Stephen." Roberta jabbed her plastic glass in Stephen's direction. Alice took it and passed it behind her to Moira.

"Maybe if Roberta has a few more she will shut up for the rest of the trip," Madeline whispered to Tom.

"Unlikely. I've seen her drunk. More like a cornered badger."

"That unpleasant, huh?" Madeline asked. Tom nodded. They sat back and watched the party scene.

"I don't need red wine spilled in my lap, Roberta, thank you very much," huffed Moira as Roberta yet again waved her glass for a refill. A drop of red wine had spilled out, narrowly missing her skirt.

"Then, move!" Roberta barked.

"Certainly not," said Stephen. "I will simply take Roberta's sadly empty glass and fill it well away from your lovely and tasteful dress. And may I say that you are dressed to perfection as always, Moira." She smiled at him in response and refluffed her hair with her long fingernails.

"Rosemary, do you care for a glass of wine?" asked Stephen. She was sitting two rows directly in front of him next to Gunter.

"No thanks, Stephen. You know I don't drink."

"Oh, give me a break. You don't drink like I don't breathe. You're a lush, and everybody in three states knows it, Ro." Roberta sipped her wine.

"And you know very well I meant that I do not drink on the bus. I get motion sickness."

"Oh, yeah. I remember. That was a mess," Elizabeth added.

"Hey, everybody! Have some cheese and crackers. I bought it at this great Italian store at lunchtime. I had them cut it into cubes to make it easier to eat," Jake yelled.

"Thanks," said Elizabeth as she took the container of cheese and crackers. "On party days, I always feel like I could use an extra hand," she said as she took the cheese with her right hand, while holding her wine in her left. She had passed the container of gazpacho to Matt, her seatmate.

"Yeah. Remember when we tried to set up that makeshift table?" Brian asked.

"Oh, yes! And when the bus swerved all the food fell off and made a mess," Fern added.

They all laughed.

"Yeah, and pain in the ass Martha insisted it blocked the way to the lav," Roberta added.

"Well, it did block it, and that one old woman was sick," Alice said.

"This is a bus not an ambulance. Stay home if you're going to be sick," Roberta barked.

Food began to appear from all sides, and it all changed hands rapidly and began to disappear as if attacked by a swarm of locusts. The regulars had become as adept as jugglers, holding their glasses in their teeth or between their legs as they put food on their plates, or balancing their food on their laps while they drank and passed food to the next person, all while the bus pitched and swayed.

"Oh, oh, oh! I don't like this salsa. It's too hot!" Moira handed it off to Stephen and moved on to the guacamole.

"The salsa is spicy, but not so much so that it is a problem for me. I must admit that I rather like it," said Stephen.

"Oh, but this bean dip is delicious. Who brought this? Can I get the recipe?" asked Brian.

"Sure, I'll be happy to share it with you," said Tony with a smirk. "It comes in a can. In fact, the attractive serving dish is the can, and you can heat it in the can too. Let me know if you need any other helpful household hints."

"Always the big spender, Tony! A can of bean dip! Hope you didn't use all your lunch money for the week," Roberta cackled.

"Wow! This salsa dip is hotter than hell!" Brian said as he passed it to Alice, his seatmate.

"Oh dear! Oh dear!" Alice was apparently in some distress. She alternated between fanning her tongue and drinking water. "Oh my gosh! That dip is too spicy hot for me." Tears welled up in her eyes. Matt reached over and grabbed the salsa from her.

"You are such a wimp!" Roberta barked at Alice. "Bringing vegetables and yogurt dip to our Mexican party. *Stupid* doesn't even begin to describe you." Roberta laughed at Alice's shocked expression and then reached around the seat in front of her and grabbed the salsa and the bag of chips from Matt.

"Hey, I was trying to eat some of that, Roberta!"

"It is probably too spicy for you too. My turn." Roberta cackled, straightened herself in her seat and took a big scoop of salsa on her chip. "If there is anything wrong with this salsa, it is too damn mild. Isn't it, Fern?" Fern nodded in agreement, while chewing an overly large piece of cheese. "In fact, I think it could be spicier. Fern, where'd I put my bag? It's not up here." Roberta was rummaging around in the overhead compartment directly above her seat, having deposited the chips and salsa with Alice who looked upset at the dip being so close to her.

"Our side was full, Robbie, so you put it on the other side," Fern reminded her.

"Oh, yeah. That was Matt's fault for being late with my bag." Roberta retrieved her green Harrods tote from the bin and removed a small plastic food-storage container. She opened it and dumped chopped jalapeño and habanero peppers into the remaining salsa. The bus lurched to a sudden stop. As Roberta clutched the seat back to keep from falling, she dropped the empty container, and it rolled down the aisle toward the front.

"Damn stupid driving, Martha!" Roberta yelled as she sat down and began to stir the salsa with a chip. "There. Now it's spicy," she pronounced as she shoveled it into her mouth. "Anybody want to try some really hot salsa? Or are you all wimps?" she said in challenge.

"Let me try it, Robbie," Fern said. Roberta passed her the dip. She took a small amount of it and didn't seem to have any problem with the spice. She looked thoughtful for a second. "As usual, the amount of peppers overwhelm everything, so it needs my special spice mix now." She took a small container out of her purse and poured in its light-colored contents. She stirred it with a chip, tasted a good amount, nodded in approval and then gave it back to Roberta. Roberta ate some, nodded her approval. She stuck two large tortilla chips in it and passed it behind her to Jake.

"Here you go! I even put chips in it for you wusses."

Jake immediately passed it to Tony, who looked warily into the red dip as if he expected something to crawl out. "That is some spicy salsa now, I bet. Fern, I can't believe you and Roberta actually bring additional ingredients to make food hotter. How can you take the heat?"

"Robbie and I eat this brand all the time, so we know what it needs to make it taste just right. I just added some minced garlic, spices and a tiny bit of salt."

Suddenly, the bus swerved into the left lane causing all the passengers to sway violently while struggling to maintain a grip on their food and drink.

"Uh oh, Tony! You spilled some salsa on your shirt." Moira pointed at the red spot on his white shirt.

"Oh, shit. Olivia will kill me." He began to wipe it with a handkerchief he pulled from his suit-jacket pocket. "I bet it will it eat a hole in my shirt." He poked at the dip with one of the chips. "Take this, will ya?" he said as he shoved the offending food at Jake.

"I have water. Maybe it will help," Madeline said holding a small bottle of water over the back of his seat.

"Okay, thanks," said Tony. He put water on his handkerchief and began to work on the spot.

"Who wants this now?" Jake asked as he held the salsa out in front of him.

"I'll take it." Roberta retrieved the tortilla chips from Alice and proceeded to finish the salsa without bothering to offer it to anyone else.

Hic...hic...hic. The noise was coming from Alice.

"Oh, for Christ's sake! Shut the hell up with those! Hold your breath or something. We have enough to annoy us without you starting up." Roberta glared at Alice.

"It's okay. She can't help it that she gets hiccups," said Brian.

"You are such a simpleminded jerk," snapped Roberta.

Brian's normally genial expression became rigid and stern as he stared back at Roberta. "Here, Alice. Drink some water from the back of the glass while you hold your breath and put your head down to your knees," Brian suggested.

"That should keep her busy for a while," Tom whispered to Madeline.

It was not long before all the food and wine were consumed, and everyone quieted down. Roberta made a point of moving into the first available free seat, which opened up in front of Gunter and Rosemary as people got off at earlier stops. She stumbled and swayed as she walked down the aisle to the free seat, grasping the seat backs as she went.

"That was a good party. Time for a nap," she said with a slur in her speech, as she flopped into a seat and tucked her feet up beside her. Other people, including some of the regulars, also spread out to vacated seats.

"It looks as though the party is over," Tom said.

"Yes. But it was entertaining while it lasted. I think Roberta must have drunk quite a bit of wine. She seemed unsteady on her feet," Madeline observed.

"Yes. It looks like she passed out."

"Well, if that is the case, we should offer her endless alcohol and food every afternoon," Madeline suggested.

CHAPTER 12

Moira rose from her seat as the bus waited for the Cross Keys Light to change in order to make a right turn down Franklin. The afternoon stop was not in front of the library, since that would block the afternoon rush-hour traffic, but three blocks farther west in front of the Pit Stop Gas 'n Go, the local gas station and convenience store. Joey picked her up at the bus stop, and she liked to get off promptly so everybody could witness Joey's attentiveness. Her bangled arm jingled as she gathered her bag from the overhead storage. "Well, guys, it's been real. This party was the most festive in quite some time. Have a nice evening," she said to all the regulars in general. Then she began to walk carefully toward the front of the bus holding onto the overhead handrail for support. She stopped short as she almost tripped over Roberta's feet, which were now sticking out into the aisle.

"Sweet Jesus! Excuse me, Roberta. I need to get by," Moira said with an annoyed tone.

Roberta didn't move or respond.

"Please move. You know my Joey's waiting." But Roberta didn't wake up. "What the hell is wrong with you?" she said in a raised voice and leaned over and attempted to shake her awake.

"Roberta! Roberta!" she screeched at the top of her lungs.

Martha stepped on the brake. "What the hell is going on back there?" she yelled.

"It's Roberta. Something's wrong." Moira stood staring down at her with an expression of shock on her face. "I think she's dead!"

All the regulars plus Tom and Madeline moved to converge on the seat in question. Martha had to push through the crowd to get a good look. Roberta was indeed dead. There was no doubt about it. She lay awkwardly across the seat, unnaturally still, with her chin resting on her chest, one arm above her head and leaning on the armrest, the other hanging straight down toward the floor and her eyes wide open behind her large glasses. There was a slightly bluish tinge to her lips. There was complete silence for a few seconds, and then everybody started to talk at once.

Fern pushed to the front of the crowd. As soon as she saw the body, her hands went to her face and she burst into tears. "No! Oh, no. Robbie! Oh, Robbie! She can't be dead. She just can't be. How? Why?"

"I'll move the bus to the Pit and call the police," Martha stated firmly.

Tom followed Martha to the front of the bus. "I think you better announce that nobody should touch anything around Roberta, and nobody can leave until the police get here." She nodded and did so once she had parked.

The driver stepped off the bus to call the police and the bus dispatcher, closing the door firmly behind her.

Fern continued to wail, almost drowning out Alice's continuing hiccups.

Tony hid his face in his hands. "I can't stand the noise. Please make it all stop," he moaned.

Jake attempted to calm Fern, but she disintegrated into a body-shaking burst of tears, punctuated with howls of despair. Moira gave Fern a lace handkerchief from her knockoff Gucci bag. "There, there now, dear. I know that this is very distressing, but please shut the hell up."

"This is indeed shocking, but we must all be as calm and patient as possible. It will all be over soon enough, I am sure," said Stephen.

Tom looked uncharacteristically grim as his brown eyes narrowed. He walked back and asked Madeline for her blanket, which he used to cover the body, and then returned to stand near the door, facing the remaining passengers.

Martha reappeared. "Okay, folks. You all have to stay and wait until the Cross Keys police get here. So just get comfortable. We will be here a while."

There was a general hum of discontent from all of the passengers. Some in the front wanted to know why they had to stay since they were not sitting near the dead woman and had not interacted with her at all.

"What do you mean I have to wait on this bus? This is my stop, and my Joey is waiting for me," Moira whined and pointed out the window to a puzzled-looking husband.

Madeline couldn't sit still any longer and went to join Tom at the front. They heard a knock and turned to see a young police officer holding a bicycle. "Although he looks like a teenager, he must be older," said Madeline.

"Yeah. Assuming some sort of age requirement, the police kid must be in his twenties at least. You'd think they would send a more experienced officer," said Martha as she opened the door.

Tom pulled out his phone. "I'll give Billy a call."

The policeman parked his bike and got on the bus. "Good evening, folks. I'm Officer John Smithfield." He smiled brightly at the passengers, who stared back at him with unhappy faces. Martha explained the situation to him. He nodded, and his expression became more serious. "Please stay calm. The chief is on the way."

"Can't we at least get off the bus? I don't want to sit on this bus with a dead body," one of the passengers said.

"I understand, and I know you folks are stressed by the unpleasant event, but a sudden death is a serious matter, and we have to examine the situation. It shouldn't take too long." Officer Smithfield looked hopefully at the door to see if help was indeed arriving.

"Oh, I feel sick," moaned Fern, and she began to whimper. Brian had moved to sit next to her and attempted to calm her, but she once again disintegrated into a burst of tears and body-wracking sobs. Black mascara ran in streaks down her cheeks.

Hic...hic...hic. Alice could still not control her hiccups.

Tony was getting restless and stood up in the aisle by his seat to stretch his legs. "Please hurry up and check out the situation. We all want to go home," he said impatiently.

Officer Smithfield slowly walked toward the back. "So, where is the deceased?"

"Right there with the blanket over her head." Matt stood up and pointed at Roberta.

Smithfield moved to the indicated seat. He gingerly pulled back the blanket to confirm the situation. He quickly dropped the blanket back in place and turned to Tom who had followed him. "Do you know her name?"

"Roberta Carlson."

He took out his notebook and wrote it down.

There was not generally much excitement in Cross Keys, and after the town's two police cars arrived with sirens blaring and lights flashing followed by an ambulance, it did not take long for a crowd of curious citizens to form next to the bus.

"What happened?" Billy said after he pushed his way through the crowd to the door where the driver and the young officer were standing.

"Chief, there's a dead woman on the bus," Smithfield said quickly. "Her name is Roberta Carlson."

Billy looked shocked. "You must be kidding me!"

"Come and see," Martha said pushing the door open. Some of the curious bystanders tried to climb aboard also, but she glared at them and pushed them back. "Seriously, you think you are going to get on my bus?" she said as she closed the door firmly.

Billy walked to the back of the bus and picked up the blanket to look at the body. He examined it for obvious wounds. "So, what exactly happened?"

"A group of daily commuters had a party," Martha said. "There was food and wine. It started around five and ended about forty-five minutes to an hour later. Nothing else happened. When we got to the Cross Keys stop around six thirty, Roberta was discovered dead in her seat."

"Did she appear sick? Complain about pain?"

"Not that I noticed," Stephen said. "She just took a nap after the party. I myself napped and did not hear or see anything." He looked around at the group as he spoke.

"Yeah, I was napping too," Tony added, and Jake nodded.

"So, were all of you asleep after the party?" The group nodded.

"Does anybody feel sick? There's an ambulance here if you need help." He addressed this to the group, all of whom said they felt fine.

"Okay. I need everybody's name and contact information, what kind of food or drink you brought to the party, what you ate and, more importantly, what you did not eat, and then you can all go home."

An hour later, Tom and Madeline stood in front of the Pit.

"What do you think happened?" Madeline asked.

Tom shrugged. "I don't know. I'm not sure... I feel something isn't right—" He stopped himself. "She probably had a heart attack or stroke while she napped. These things do happen," he said finally.

"It's shocking. She was not that old."

"True. But at least she died in her sleep."

"That's something, anyway. It just seems so...odd."

Tom nodded. "Sudden death is always disturbing. I better get to the bar."

"Okay. Have a good weekend."

"You too."

CHAPTER 13

Soon after, Billy had performed the difficult task of informing her sister of Roberta's sudden death. Samantha greeted him pleasantly and showed him into the kitchen, where they sat down at the table. She was devastated by the news. "Robbie hated doctors. She was never sick. But something must have been wrong. If only she—" She broke down. Then she stood up and began to busy herself, making coffee and unwrapping cookies as tears ran down her face.

She finally composed herself and sat down again at the table. Billy reached over and put his hand on her shoulder to comfort her.

"I realize it must be quite a shock. It is difficult enough to lose a loved one, but sudden death is especially hard. Had she been ill recently?" Samantha shook her head. "Did she have any chronic health issues, such a heart problem or high blood pressure?"

"No. Like I said, she was never sick. That's what makes it so hard to believe. She didn't have a single prescription medication. She hated drugs and doctors. She never even took an aspirin. I take a handful of pills each day, but not her."

Billy nodded in understanding and they discussed various aspects of Roberta and her doctor and drug phobias.

"Was she under any new stress? At work or personally?"

"Not that I was aware of. Actually, she seemed happier than normal. For her that meant she was less offensive in her dealings with people in general."

"Okay. Thank you for your time." Billy stood. "We would like to perform an autopsy to determine the cause of her passing, if that is all right with you."

"Thank you, Billy. I would appreciate it."

"And I may have additional questions later. But as of now, I don't think there is anything to investigate."

Samantha nodded. "I understand. You have been very kind and efficient."

"That would have shocked Roberta, huh?" He smiled at her as she nodded her head in agreement. "I'll stop by with the results as soon as I have them."

* * *

News of Roberta's sudden death sped through the Cross Keys grapevine. Harry and Jeff were eager to hear all the details from Madeline during their weekend dinner. She explained that it was really extremely dull; she died quietly while sleeping in her seat. There was nothing to tell.

"There are only a few people in town who are sad to hear about Roberta's death. I've never seen anything like it," Harry said.

"Are people going to avoid sitting in that seat?" Jeff asked.

"Yes, the seat of death! Haunted by the unmourned victim," Harry added.

"Don't scare Maddie. She has to ride on that bus every day!" Jeff scolded. He turned to her. "Thinking about Roberta haunting you is dreadful. Just dreadful."

"You're right. She wouldn't be Casper, she would be a poltergeist," Harry said laughing and made a spooky sound.

Madeline laughed too. "Well, the seat didn't kill her, so I don't think the bus is going to be haunted. As far as we know, she died of natural causes. At least, that's what Tom thinks. Probably massive indigestion based on what she ate. It was strange, though. She certainly seemed strong and healthy in addition to mean."

"How did the other passengers take it?" Jeff asked.

Madeline shrugged her shoulders. "They were shocked, and Fern was upset. There really is nothing to tell."

"This is so disappointing. I was hoping for more drama," he added.

"Actually, there will probably be less drama now without Roberta's constant stream of insults."

"So, what's happening with you and Tom?" Harry asked.

"Nothing is happening. We are just bus buddies," Madeline said firmly, avoiding eye contact.

Harry and Jeff exchanged a conspiratorial look. "I always find the rugged, handsome type attractive," Harry said.

"How do you think I attracted this one?" Jeff said.

Madeline blushed in embarrassment. "Well, don't hold your breath. He's a pretty complicated guy, and I don't think he is interested in a romantic relationship. At least not with me."

CHAPTER 14

Billy walked into The Opossum midafternoon on Saturday a week after Roberta's death. Since it was between lunch and happy hour, the bar was empty except for the perpetual barflies clustered at a table near the fireplace.

"Hey, Billy," Adam greeted him. "Can I get you something?"

"I will take a cup of coffee. Tom around?" Billy asked as he stood at the bar.

"He's down in the cellar changing kegs. I'll get him."

When Tom appeared, he poured himself a cup of coffee and stood next to Billy and gave him an appraising glance. "You look like there is something on your mind."

Billy looked sheepish. "Can we go up to your office? I don't want to run the risk of being overheard."

Once in the office, Billy flopped down on the love seat with a sigh. "I have a bit of news on Roberta's death."

"The autopsy report came in?"

Billy nodded and sighed. "Turns out she did not die of natural causes. She died from a drug overdose."

"Really?" Tom looked shocked as he sat down in his desk chair. "What specifically?"

"A combination of oxycodone and benzodiazepines, like Xanax. Unfortunately, it's a common deadly combination."

"Oh, I see. But from the expression on your face, I assume she wasn't prescribed any of these drugs?"

"Not according to her sister, Samantha. She says Roberta never took any pills. Not even an aspirin. She told me that when I told her about Roberta's death. I asked about Roberta's general health and medications. She said Roberta was phobic about medication, thought the side effects did more harm than the drug did good, and she also had a phobia about swallowing pills. Thought she was going to choke."

"How did Samantha take the news?"

"She was shocked. She said there was no way Roberta knowingly took that stuff. She said point-blank that somebody killed her sister, that they poisoned her with the drugs."

Tom studied his coffee for a minute. "How quickly would the drugs work?"

"Naturally, depends on the individual. But based on the amount in her system, about twenty minutes to half an hour. The drug combo in addition to the wine, especially in somebody who doesn't take the drugs so has no resistance built up, and is as small as Roberta, well, it was deadly. She slowly stopped breathing, and her heart stopped."

"So, it had to have happened during the party."

"Yes, it had to have been in the party food. Are you sure you didn't see anything odd? Tom, this means one of the commuters killed her. Or somebody who supplied the food.

"Now I need you to tell me exactly and precisely what you saw on the day of the murder. You're my best witness. You just sat and observed. Did you see anything that might indicate who poisoned her? Anything unusual?"

"Everything was perfectly normal. Normal for the bus, I mean. I was running late that day. When I got there, most of the regulars were already on the bus, and they were set up for the party with plates and napkins. I wasn't aware there was a party planned. Apparently, they do this now and then. Makes the ride seem faster, at least to them, I guess. The last person to get on was Matt. He usually stands next to the bus and smokes until the last minute. After we got out of the tunnel, they started their party.

"I am not sure who brought what food. Some of it was home-made. I saw it passed around in Tupperware-type containers, and some was obviously purchased since it was still in the packaging." He shrugged. "I don't know for sure if everybody tasted some of everything. But I think everything was eaten. I really wasn't paying close attention to who ate what food."

"What was the conversation like?"

Tom took a sip of coffee as he thought. "The usual joking and give-and-take. Nothing comes to mind as being very significant. Other than the discussion about the spiciness of the salsa."

"What was that about?"

"Apparently the salsa dip was extremely spicy. Most people thought it was too spicy, but Roberta thought it was not spicy enough, and she added hot peppers to it—at least it looked like jalapeño peppers she had brought from home. She took the container from her tote. Fern also added something. Garlic, I think she said. I don't remember if anybody other than Fern and Roberta ate any after that."

"That may be significant. Fern tasted it after the additional ingredients were added?"

Tom looked thoughtful. "I think so. But I'm not sure. I don't think anybody but Roberta ate it after that, but I really am not sure. I know she made a big deal about finishing it. About everybody being too wimpy to eat it. Oh, and she dropped the pepper container on the floor when the bus stopped or swerved suddenly. So, I guess it is long gone. No chance of testing it for the drugs."

Billy shook his head. "Yeah. In fact, all the food containers are long gone or cleaned. Roberta's wasn't in her tote, which I turned over to Samantha. She said she couldn't face looking in it, you know, seeing all Roberta's things, so she just put it in her room. Fern mentioned she added spice but said she threw away the container."

"Odd. Or convenient." Tom paused in thought. "Now that I think about it, Roberta stumbled when she changed her seat, and her speech was slurred. Madeline and I thought she had had too much wine. So, Samantha had no idea about who on the bus would particularly want to kill her sister?"

"No. Apparently, they led separate lives in many ways. Roberta hung out with Fern, and Samantha has her own friends. They were roommates because they could afford a nicer and bigger house together."

"Does Samantha gain from Roberta's death?"

"Not that I know of at this point. I have to check on life insurance, the will and any other pertinent financial records. With the Grickly murder still open, I have two murders to solve at the same time. The mayor will be fit to be tied when she finds out. And the usual town busybodies will have plenty to say, like that blogger who thinks he's an investigative reporter. I want to keep this quiet as long as possible while I investigate. Samantha has agreed to keep it secret. Maybe the killer will get comfortable, think we don't know and make a mistake."

"Just a matter of time, I guess, before somebody gets wind of it and spreads it all over town."

They sat in silence for a few seconds. Finally, Billy said, "I'll keep digging. Let me know if you think of *anything* else. But please keep this quiet." He got up to leave. "Oh, any luck with Grickly's ledger?"

Tom shook his head. "Afraid not. I don't think I am going to be any help to you on that."

Billy nodded. "Thanks anyway. Keep it in the back of your mind, and something might come to you."

After the chief had left, Tom sat drinking more coffee and thinking. He was flabbergasted that Roberta was poisoned. He ran over the events of the party in his mind, but nothing jumped out at him. Yet he had a strong feeling that something had happened that seemed out of place, but he could not put his finger on it. But he did know he wanted to solve this murder. It had happened right in front of him. He and Ralph had always reasoned through complex cases together, bouncing ideas around. He decided to share this news with Madeline; after all, she was a witness too and had seen as much as he had. There was a chance she had noticed something he had not. And she was an outsider with no ties to Roberta or any of the other potential suspects. He really liked her and believed he could trust her to keep it quiet.

* * *

Tom hoped Madeline would show up for dinner, and sure enough she walked through the door at her usual time. Now he didn't have to wait until Monday to talk to her.

"Hi. I'm glad you stopped by tonight," he said to her with a serious tone that disconcerted her.

"Uh, me too," she said, giving him a bemused look. "It's been a while, and I need a good burger."

"And you still came here!" Tom smiled.

"Not everybody uses real opossum in their burgers, you know."

"I need to speak with you privately for a minute." He sounded serious again.

"Sure," she said a bit taken aback. "What's up?"

"We better sit in the back."

He led her to a corner table, and Adam followed with drinks. Tom looked at her with a stern expression. "Can I trust you to keep a secret?"

"Certainly."

"This is very secret. You can't tell anyone. That includes Harry and Jeff." Madeline nodded in agreement. "Billy came by this afternoon and told me that Roberta was poisoned."

Her eyes widened in astonishment. "What!" She sat in silence staring blankly at Tom. "Oh my God! How?" she finally blurted out.

"A lethal combination of opioids and Xanax."

"But I didn't see Roberta take any pills. So, that means—"

"She never took pills of any kind, according to her sister. She had a phobia about them. The drugs that killed her were crushed up and added to the food. One of the commuters could be a murderer. I was thinking we could figure out how it was done and who did it," Tom said as he looked at her intently.

"We?" Madeline looked surprised. She was flattered he had asked for her help. "Okay, I guess. But that doesn't sound like it will be easy to do, and anyway aren't the police working on it?"

"Of course. But we were the only ones who were there, didn't eat the party food and know all the players. Maybe we can *quietly* help Billy along."

"So, I guess you really haven't given up being a PI?"

Tom smiled. "Old habits die hard."

"I don't know, Tom. It makes me nervous. It'll be bad enough to ride the bus now, with a possible murderer so close." Madeline was being truthful, but she was torn for other reasons. She really wanted to work with him, thinking this could bring them closer, but she was not sure she would be helpful, which might cause him to think less of her.

"I understand." Tom looked and sounded disappointed. He began to stand.

Madeline put her hand gently on his arm. "But wait. If we can help swiftly solve the case and make everyone safer, I guess we should try. So, I'll help. But we need to keep it strictly between us. I don't want to become a target."

"Absolutely," he said and smiled as he settled back into his chair. "I don't want you, or me for that matter, to get hurt. Samantha and I are the only people Billy shared the information with. And it would be best for now if he doesn't know I told you. Billy asked Samantha to keep it quiet while he searches for the killer. He knows it won't stay secret for long, and he's trying to get as far as he can while he still has the element of surprise."

Madeline nodded in agreement. "When do you want to start?"

"How about tomorrow morning? We can meet here in my office, away from all the gossips and prying eyes. You bring donuts, and I'll make the coffee."

"Like real police, huh? Now, can I get my burger? I am really hungry."

"Certainly. The opossum is fresh tonight!"

"Sounds scrumptious!"

CHAPTER 15

Madeline knocked on the locked bar door late Sunday morning. She looked up and down the alley, but nobody was in sight. The only sound was the squeak of the swaying sign over her head. She felt like a spy but figured they probably didn't show up to clandestine meetings with egg sandwiches and donuts from the diner. Tom answered her knock almost immediately and took her up to his office, where he had set up an old reversible blackboard on wheels, on which he had drawn the bus-seating arrangement.

Eliz & Matt	*Ro & Gun*
Fern & Roberta	*Alice & Brian*
Tony & Jake	*Moira & Stephen*
Mad & Tom	*Lavatory*

Madeline looked around the office for photos or any other personal items that might give her more insight into Tom. But there was nothing. He obviously used the space just for bar business; it wasn't a refuge or favorite spot.

"Aren't you old school with your nifty blackboard," Madeline quipped.

Tom gave her a questioning look. "You were expecting a PowerPoint presentation, I presume?"

"A least a modern whiteboard with colorful markers."

"I guess I could get colored chalk."

They sat side by side on the love seat staring at the blackboard and eating donuts and drinking coffee.

"This seems impossible. They all ate the same food, and it was passed around to everybody," Madeline finally said.

"I know."

"Did they test any of the food containers for the drugs?"

Tom shook his head. "Good question. No. The fact it was a murder was discovered too late. All the physical evidence is gone. We have to narrow the suspect pool down to the most likely people. Then maybe we can figure out how it was done and close in on the killer."

Madeline looked dubious. "Okay...I guess. Sounds straightforward but difficult. Using the diagram, I think we can eliminate Gunter, Rosemary, Elizabeth, Moira, Stephen and Brian. And, of course, Fern."

"Why do you pick them for elimination?"

"Gunter, Rosemary, Elizabeth and Brian are not solid clique members. I think of them as a satellite group. She didn't pick on them as often as she did the others. Fern because she was Roberta's so-called best friend. Basically, that leaves the people I think of as the core group. I don't think Alice is really a core member. But sitting right across the aisle gave her both a good view of what Roberta was doing and access to her. So, we are down to the people she picked on the most or who sat near her."

Tom looked impressed. "You're good at this."

"Well, I did take forensic accounting for two semesters. That is kind of like solving a mystery."

"That leaves us with Matt, Alice, Tony and Jake. However, I would add Fern as a potential suspect. Sometimes best friends can become best enemies, and she was Roberta's seatmate. So that is our suspect pool. Now we need to establish each person's possible motive."

Madeline looked unsure. "I don't know. Fern was very upset on the bus that night. Do you think that could have been an act? If so, she should be an actor. I was convinced."

Tom shrugged. "I really don't know Fern all that well. There may be depths to her shallow personality that I don't know about. Roberta ordered her around all the time and obviously knew a lot of personal details about her life. Maybe she just got sick of it."

"Hm. Maybe." Madeline sat with her chin on her hand, lost in thought for a moment. "So, what food would the poison be in? Not the yogurt dip and crudités, nor the cheese and crackers. It had to be the bean dip, nachos, guacamole or salsa. Or maybe the wine. Roberta drank enough of that, right?"

"Yes, it had to have a strong flavor to mask the crushed-up drugs. So, I think the wine is out."

Madeline looked at him closely. "Hmm. I think you may have a plausible theory about the food."

"I think it was the spicy salsa."

"Oh, yes! I forgot! Fern and Roberta both added spicy seasonings they'd brought with them. And nobody wanted to eat it after that," Madeline said excitedly and sat back on the love seat. "Actually, nobody wanted to eat it before, either. But Roberta wouldn't poison herself, and Fern, most likely, wouldn't poison her best friend."

"Not knowingly," Tom said.

"What are you thinking?"

"Someone may have doctored the ingredients without Roberta or Fern knowing. In any case, the murderer was willing to run the risk of killing somebody other than the intended victim. They had no control over who was going to eat the salsa or how much would be eaten at a time. They must have an extremely strong motive."

"Well, if two people died, then not knowing who the intended victim was would just confuse the issue and maybe even make it easier to get away with the murder."

"But two deaths would have definitely triggered an investigation," Tom noted.

"Hey! Are we even sure Roberta was the intended victim?"

"Oh, I think that is a safe assumption, knowing her as we did."

"But who would have access to the additional items?" Madeline asked. "Could it be someone other than one of the regulars? That really muddies the water."

Tom shrugged. "Maybe. We need to keep our minds open to the possibility. Right now, we need to find out who from our group wanted Roberta dead and why."

"How are we going to find out who wanted her dead? We can't just ask the regulars. Who'll talk to us? I wouldn't."

Tom looked at her in surprise. "My, you're getting a bit cynical, aren't you?"

"Having a cheating husband does that to a girl."

"We have to ask the right questions when we can and listen all the time."

They sat silently on the love seat and stared at the blackboard, thinking.

"Roberta's viewing is tomorrow evening at the funeral home," Tom said.

"I didn't really know her. I would feel awkward going to her viewing. Why did it take so long to have the viewing and funeral?"

"It took time to get the body back from the autopsy. We need to attend the viewing. I think we might have a good chance of finding out something there."

"Is that an old PI trick?"

"The oldest in the book. People let their guard down at wakes and funerals."

"Do I have to cry?" she asked as she bit into a donut.

"No more than anybody else."

CHAPTER 16

The Perkins-Perry Funeral Home was located at the western edge of town on Franklin Street. As with many buildings in Cross Keys, it had been repurposed from its previous grandeur. In this case, it had been a small, elite hotel featuring suites with a receiving room and separate bedrooms; in addition, it had servants' quarters, so the wealthy could bring along domestic help. It was an imposing dark Gothic structure, which was perfectly suited for its current use.

Madeline had no idea what to expect and was surprised to find that, once inside, it was welcoming, with subtle lighting, comfortable chairs and sofas, and side tables with boxes of tissues. The walls had pale pink and ivory floral wallpaper, while the floor was covered with a thick neutral carpet, which dampened sound. She felt awkward showing up to Roberta's viewing, since she was not a relative or close friend, so she was pleased to see that Tom was already there. He had abandoned his usual jeans for gray slacks and a white button-down shirt and a sports jacket.

The casket was open and surrounded by vases full of white roses. There was a large open-wreath standing spray of all-white flowers, including lilies, mums and snapdragons.

White roses and white flowers in general must have been Roberta's favorites, Madeline gathered.

She was surprised at the number of people filling the sizable visitation room. "Wow," she whispered to Tom, "I thought there would not be many people here. I mean, since she was so hateful and nasty to everybody in general."

"Perhaps they want to be sure she is dead."

"Very funny."

They stood side by side at the wall by the entrance so they could see everything. "Lots of flowers. That's a surprise," Madeline observed.

Tom shrugged. "In my experience, people tend to be generous for the benefit of the family. Not necessarily because they loved the deceased," he said.

"Hm, I see. So, we are just going to stand here and eavesdrop and watch?"

"Yes."

Fern was sitting in a corner crying, with a box of tissues on her lap. Jake was sitting next to her and would occasionally pat her softly on the arm or shoulder. Moira arrived dressed all in black and pulling Joey behind her as she walked up to view the body. She dabbed her eyes with a lacy white handkerchief. Stephen, Ro and Elizabeth stood in a group near Fern and Jake looking uncomfortable.

Matt came in, took a quick look around the room and walked promptly up to a pretty, tall, slender woman with long light brown hair. She turned with a smile, but when she saw it was Matt, she looked annoyed, and after a short conversation, he left her and sat down on the other side of Fern.

"Is that Matt's wife?" Madeline asked Tom.

"Yes, that's Kate. And the woman who just stood up in the front row is Roberta's sister, Samantha." The woman Tom indicated with a tilt of his head looked very much like Roberta, but a little plumper, with a pleasant expression on her face, a more flattering hairstyle and trendy glasses. When she smiled, she showed perfect white teeth and dimples in her full cheeks. She greeted people with real warmth.

"Do you think Roberta once had dimples? Before she forgot how to smile, that is. Her sister doesn't seem too upset," Madeline said.

"Well, can you blame her? It must have been hell actually living with Roberta."

"Maybe she takes medication? Could it be oxy or benzos?" Madeline suggested.

"Hmm. That's a thought."

When they turned their attention back to the bus group, Tony had arrived with a beautiful dark-haired woman wearing an expensive navy blue designer dress. She was impeccably groomed from head to toe, her deep brown eyes were ringed with long lashes, and her full lips were bright red, setting off her flawless pale complexion.

She never spoke to anyone but smiled condescendingly at the group and generally seemed annoyed to be there.

"I assume that is Tony's wife?"

"Yes, that is Olivia. I am surprised she showed up."

Moira stopped to speak to various people on her way back to the rear of the room. She noticed Madeline and Tom and walked up to them. "It was nice of you two to come, considering you haven't been on the bus for long."

"It seemed like the right thing to do. It must be sad for you. I mean, it is sad to lose someone you've known for so long," Madeline said.

"Oh yes, dear, you are so right. Roberta and I knew each other for ages. Of course, she was not everybody's cup of tea. She, unlike myself, was a big gossip and a troublemaker." Moira nodded thoughtfully. "Take Matt, for instance. He blames Roberta for his pending divorce. Now, isn't that just like a man? Refusing to take any responsibility for his own misdeeds."

"How was Roberta involved in Matt's separation?"

Moira moved closer and lowered her voice. "Matt lost all their money. It was some get-rich-quick scheme that failed miserably. They were going to lose their home and were about to declare bankruptcy. So, Roberta lent them money to keep them afloat and in the house. Matt's wife is Roberta's cousin—she's over there." Moira pointed at Kate.

"Kate and Roberta were very close. According to Matt, Roberta charged a high interest rate and expected her payment on the first of the month without fail. She really had them over a barrel. So, that pressure together with Matt's foolishness was more than Kate could take, and she threw him to the curb. But really, things had not been honeymoon-happy for quite some time. It seems that she would cry on Roberta's shoulder about her marital problems, and Roberta encouraged her to stand on her own two feet."

"You mean, she encouraged Kate to leave Matt?"

Moira fanned her hands in the air, which caused her bracelets to jingle. "To put it bluntly, yes. Roberta encouraged her to take the children and leave rather than attempt to work things out. You know how it is. That can take forever. And Matt is no prize, you know. A sales rep for some no-name copier-machine company. He doesn't make a lot of money and doesn't have a bright future, I would guess. She felt Kate deserved more and needed to move on and find a better man."

"Matt wanted to work things out?"

"Oh, heavens, yes. He was very upset. He wanted his family and happy home back."

They noticed Samantha approaching the bus group, and the three of them moved to join them. Matt stood up, but Fern and Jake remained seated. Samantha surveyed the group with a sad expression on her face. "Thank you all for coming. I know Roberta would have appreciated it."

"It was the least we could do," Moira spoke for the group. "It was a shock to us all."

"Yes. An enormous shock to me too. She was so healthy. She never even got a cold. This is a lesson to us all that we can go at any time, I guess." Samantha's voice shook as her eyes filled with tears, and she struggled to hold them back. Finally, she shrugged her shoulders and sighed.

"When is the funeral?" Elizabeth asked.

"There's not going to be a funeral. Roberta always said she never wanted one. She will be cremated, and I will have a remembrance get-together at the house soon. I will certainly let you all know what day and time. Thank you all again for coming. It means so much to me." She turned to leave and gave a quick glance to Billy, who nodded at her. He had been standing still and quiet against the wall opposite the door.

A wail of despair erupted from Fern. Jake put his arm around her and patted her gently. The rest of the group stood in silence and looked appropriately sad.

Olivia tugged on Tony's arm insistently and finally he agreed to leave. Moira and Joey soon followed. Jake continued to sit with Fern, while Matt sat next to them and stared glumly at his wife across the room.

Tom and Madeline moved back to their observation point. Billy came up to them.

"Didn't think I'd see you here," the chief said.

"It seemed like the decent thing to do, since I was on the bus when she died. You remember Madeline?"

"Yes, nice to see you again."

"Yes, too bad it is under these circumstances. How is your hand?"

"Oh, it's fine now. Thanks for asking."

"Well, it has been a long day, and I need to get to the bar," Tom said.

"Yes, I took the late bus and haven't even been home yet," Madeline added.

Tom and Madeline left the funeral home and walked east on Franklin.

"That was interesting. You were right about us needing to be there," Madeline said.

"Glad you agree. Oh, and good work getting Moira to gossip about Matt."

"I discovered early on she is a great source of information."

"We need to go over our information again. I am not going to be on the bus for the next two days. Do you want to come to the bar after work tomorrow? I am thinking of adding pizza to the menu, so we could do a taste test."

"Sure. Sounds good." They walked in silence for few minutes. "Samantha did a good job of behaving as if nothing was wrong when she greeted the bus group, didn't she?" Tom nodded in agreement. "If Stephen isn't on the bus tomorrow, I can sit next to Moira and maybe find out more about our other suspects."

"Good idea. Okay, I'll see you tomorrow," Tom said as he turned into the alley.

CHAPTER 17

The next day, the regulars were subdued. Seeing Roberta's lifeless body and facing the suddenness of her death reminded everybody that life was short and they were spending way too much of their limited time on a bus. Fern and Tom were not there, so Madeline decided to sit in Roberta's seat, as it put her in the middle of the group where she could hear everything.

"Poor Fern," Moira said. "She must be lost without Roberta."

"Yeah, now she has no one to tell her what to do," Matt said. "I'd feel free if I was her."

"Shut up, Matt! We know you hated her," Alice said. "She's grieving for her best friend. Have a little respect."

"Well, I for one do not miss her, and I bet I am not the only one," he said.

"The bus will certainly be more civil without her," Elizabeth added.

"I agree with Matt. I don't miss her," Jake yelled. "She caused me a ton of trouble for no reason."

"It is not right to speak ill of the dead," Alice objected in a strident tone.

"We do have this idea, or superstition really, that we cannot speak ill of the dead," Stephen said. "But isn't it obvious most of us disliked her intimidating manner and nasty comments? We really have nothing nice to say about her. It is hard to feel sorry she is gone."

"Was she always belligerent?" Madeline asked.

"Yes!" the group responded in unison.

"The only quiet ride we ever had with Roberta on the bus was when she had laryngitis from yelling her head off at a basketball game," Tony said.

"I agree. It will be a more pleasant ride without her," Brian added.

"So, none of you are saddened by her death?"

"Well, no, Madeline. She either verbally assaulted each of us or actually did something vindictive to us," Stephen explained without giving any details.

"Or both," Tony added. "The truth is that Fern is the only one who will miss her."

Madeline attempted to draw out more information, but the subject had come to its natural conclusion. Nobody wanted to continue to relive Roberta's bullying and obnoxious comments. She spent the remainder of the ride staring out the window and thinking about whom among the group was the most likely murderer. She couldn't decide.

* * *

Adam greeted Madeline as she walked up to the bar. "Tom's in his office. He said for you to go up and join him." He rushed by to deliver beers to two men at the end of the bar.

She walked up the steep stairs to find the office door open. Tom was sitting on the love seat studying the blackboard, his brow furrowed in thought. She thought she had never seen a more handsome man.

"Looks like you are thinking hard. Any new ideas?" she asked as she walked in and dropped her coat and bus bag on one of the desk chairs.

Tom looked up at her and smiled. "Hi. How was the bus?"

"Not nearly as bitchy as usual. Nobody is sorry Roberta is gone. They actually said so."

"I am not surprised. Any leads?"

"Not really. I think we need to review what we know and plan our next move."

"Okay. Well, I think we have the correct list of suspects. Our murderer had to know how Roberta habitually added ingredients to the salsa and what they were. The fact that it was unlikely anybody would eat any of it after it was doctored was probably part of their plan," Tom added.

"I see you have a nice list going on the blackboard." Madeline stood next to the board reading the list.

1. *Roberta and Fern added ingredients brought separately.*

2. *The poison could have been added to the containers without their knowledge. Who had access? Samantha at home?*

3. *Drugs were put into the salsa by one of the regulars as it was passed around. Matt, Alice, Jake or Tony?*

"Do you really think Samantha would kill her own sister?" Madeline asked after studying the points for a few moments.

"We don't know the nature of their relationship. Anything's possible at this point."

"I think Roberta cut up the peppers the night before. At four in the morning, who wants to cut things up, especially hot peppers? I know I wouldn't want to do that in addition to getting dressed for work and making it to the bus on time. That means they were probably in the refrigerator all night. That would give Samantha plenty of time to put the drugs in them. Bit of a stretch, though."

Tom nodded. "But she had to be aware of how Roberta habitually doctored the salsa. So was Fern."

They were silent for a few moments. "Matt really hated Roberta," Madeline finally said.

"We already know he had a strong motive. Owing money to Roberta must have been a special kind of hell. But I just don't see him as the killer. I don't think he has the guts for it. Stabbing her in a fit of rage with the carving knife at a family holiday dinner during an argument—I could see that happening. But this was carefully planned and took nerve to execute."

"Hmm. But sometimes the mild mannered can surprise you when they get backed into a corner. And he was definitely cornered."

"True. But she'd tortured him for a long time. Why now?"

"Not sure." They sat in silence, each studying the board. "Yeah, I agree. He seems too beaten down to do something like this. So, that leaves Tony, Jake, Alice, Fern and Samantha," Madeline finally said.

"In order to find out if any of them had a compelling reason to kill Roberta, I think we need to gossip with Moira. Your font of information."

"That is a natural pastime for her, so she won't think we are looking for something specific. Any chance we can get her to come to The Opossum and have a few cocktails? That might loosen her tongue even more."

"I will see what I can do."

"So, where is this pizza?" Madeline asked.

"It should be ready shortly. I hope you like hot peppers."

"As long as they haven't been sprinkled with deadly drugs, I am fine with them," she said, picking up her belongings.

"Well, Cook can be secretive regarding his special spices, but I think we're safe," he said as they left the office.

Instead of sitting at the bar to eat, Tom led her to a table where they sat down together. It was not busy, so Adam and Debby could easily cope with the customers.

"Do you know if Billy has made any progress?" she asked as she sipped a beer.

"Not that I know of. I'll give him a call in a day or so, if he doesn't call me, and see what I can find out."

"It must be nice to have a friend you have known your whole life. It's like having a brother—" Madeline stopped herself. "Oh, I didn't mean..."

Tom smiled. "Yes. Billy is very much like a brother to me. It is a comfort since I have no close family left. He had an unorthodox upbringing, and I was lucky enough to be included in some of the adventures. He was raised by his grandmother. She showed him the world. People think he is a bumbling, unsophisticated country police officer, but he's not."

The pizza arrived, and they ate in silence for a bit. "What do you think?" Tom asked.

"Not quite on par with New York's, but delicious."

Tom grinned. "I will pass that on to Cook."

CHAPTER 18

Billy had been thinking about both the murders all day on Monday as he went about his normal police duties, including arrests for shoplifting and domestic disputes. He replaced the chair wheel and adjusted the pillow then sat down at his small metal desk. He decided to focus on the bus murder. He knew he had to work fast before the news of the poisoning leaked. Deep in thought, waiting for the jumble of information in his head to coalesce into a theory, he placed his pencil in the middle of the desk and watched as it slowly rolled toward him.

He read over yet again all of the notes he had taken so far, and then he stared out his window at the alley that ran behind the High Street stores and the post office. He had not had a case that was so difficult to get a handle on in a long time. Normally, murder and manslaughter in Cross Keys were straightforward, if not downright stupid. The guilty party was the boyfriend or wife, the buddy who drank too much and got violently angry or created an accident, or a burglary gone wrong. Rarely did the perpetrator put any real planning or thought into the crime.

He had briefly interviewed each of the people on the bus and was now trying to figure out where to go next. He finally decided to concentrate on Alice, since she'd sat directly across the narrow aisle from Roberta that day. Sitting right in the middle of the group, she and Fern had the best chance of seeing if Roberta added anything else to her food or was passed anything nobody else was given. He felt certain the salsa had contained the drugs as its strong spices would mask the taste. Since Fern had also added ingredients to the salsa, he figured he should talk to Alice again first. He checked his watch and found that he had plenty of time for pie and coffee before the bus was due.

* * *

Alice and Andy Miller lived in a nice but less affluent neighborhood just off a high-traffic main state road. A large section of their house was under repair from an explosion and fire that Billy remembered hearing about from his friends on the volunteer fire department. There had been much speculation about the cause. It was a long wait for an answer to his knock until a shrill female voice asked, "Who's there?"

"Chief of police."

"Okay. One minute." After unlocking what seemed like ten locks, Alice opened the door.

"Sorry to disturb you, Mrs. Miller, but I need to clear up a few loose ends concerning the day of Roberta's passing."

As he stepped into the house, he was overwhelmed by the odor of cats. There were at least six in sight, and from the amount of fur on the floor, it looked like either a mountain lion or a dozen more house cats must be hiding. He began to sniffle; his nose itched, and his eyes started to water. Alice showed him into a living room that looked like a showroom window for a discount furniture store, except the sofa and recliner were both covered with cats.

"Just push a cat aside, and sit wherever you want," Alice said graciously.

Billy scratched his head in thought then attempted to move a large white cat sitting on the recliner. The cat stared at him, hissed and refused to budge.

"Not him. That's Snowball, my husband's favorite. He moves for nobody. That's his chair," Alice said as she swept five cats from the sofa and motioned for Billy to sit.

"Who's here, Alice?" her husband yelled from upstairs.

"The police," she yelled back. "He wants to speak with me about Roberta's death."

"Whose death?"

"The woman on the bus."

"Oh! Okay. I'll stay up here."

They sat in silence, while Billy gently pushed first one cat then another and another from his lap. Alice just glared at him. Billy sneezed. "Mrs. Miller, I was wondering if you could review, once again, what you saw on the bus that day. Your observations are particularly important, since you were sitting just across the aisle from the deceased during the party. I have to do this sort of due diligence to be sure we have looked at every possible scenario and give closure to the family. Many times, they have difficulty believing their loved one simply died, and they start making up reasons. I have to be sure I have all the answers for them. Can you go over once again what she ate and, to the best of your memory, the order that she ate it in?"

Alice nodded. "It's all a bit of a blur, but I can try. Roberta was like a vacuum cleaner, sucking up food faster than anyone else. It all started with the wine, of course. They always start with the alcohol. After guzzling two full glasses of wine, she started eating everything that got passed. Cheese, vegetables, soup, chips, bean dip. You name it. Then she made a big whoop-de-do of the salsa's being too mild and spiced it up so hot that only she could eat it."

Billy was writing furiously. "Thank you. That is quite comprehensive. So, other than the peppers, you didn't see Roberta add anything to any of the food?"

Alice sat in thoughtful silence staring straight ahead. "Yes," she finally said.

"Yes, she did not, or yes, she did?"

"Yes, she did."

Billy was surprised but tried to appear calm. "So, what did she add and to which food?"

"She added Tabasco to the gazpacho. The soup was passed around in a plastic juice container, you know, like Tupperware. She had a small bottle of Tabasco and she almost emptied it into the soup."

"Where did she get the Tabasco?"

"It came from Matt."

Well, hello, Billy thought to himself.

"She poked him in the shoulder with her fork." Alice continued, "Very unsanitary, if you ask me. She reminded him that she had asked him to get some for her. Then he passed something to her, and the next thing I saw was her adding the Tabasco to the gazpacho."

"How much gazpacho was left in the container at this point?"

"I don't know. Not much."

"And did she drink it?"

"Oh, yes. She drank it all."

"Did you happen to see anything else unusual?"

Alice appeared to be thinking, and she was silent for several seconds. "No," she finally said.

"Well, thanks a lot, Mrs. Miller. You have been very helpful." Billy stood up and sneezed in three short bursts. He was covered in cat hair.

"You need to take care of that cold," Alice said.

Billy just nodded and left.

* * *

They were called town houses, but they were really just small apartments in a long brick two-story building. Matt lived in number five. Billy rang the bell, and Matt answered quickly. "Good evening, Mr. O'Conner. Do you mind if I come in and ask you a few questions? I just need to tie up some loose ends about Roberta's death."

Matt looked surprised. "Loose ends? Why?"

Billy smiled. "Yes, in preparation for closing out the investigation. It's all routine, when someone dies in public, you know, I have to submit a complete report. Got to have all my bases covered. There's a mountain of paper work."

Matt nodded. "Yes, I can believe that. Come on in. I just got home and was about to eat my dinner."

"I'll be as quick as I can." Billy looked around the one-room studio. There was not much room for anything, but Matt's possessions were neat and orderly. Matt went to a convenience kitchen situated in one corner of the room and took a beer out of the undercounter refrigerator. "Want one?"

"Thanks, but I'm on duty."

Billy thought that it would be next to impossible to cook a decent meal in the tiny kitchen, with a small refrigerator, two burners and a sink with no more than two feet of counter space. Matt was eating pizza with his beer.

He sat down on the sofa, the only place to sit in the room, and motioned the chief to join him.

Billy pulled out his notebook and flipped a few pages. "It has become obvious that Roberta liked spicy food. One of your fellow passengers mentioned that you had given Roberta a small bottle of Tabasco."

Matt nodded as he continued to eat. "Yes. Roberta had called me at the office and asked me to pick some up on my way to the bus. She was held up at her office and was running late. So, I did. She asked for it during the party, and I gave it to her. Is this important?"

"Just trying to reconstruct the party as accurately as possible. You were related to Roberta by marriage?"

"Yes. She was my wife's cousin. We are separated right now."

"Does Roberta's death impact your relationship? I understand you went to see your wife the night she died."

"Yes. How did you know that?"

"General information from your bus friends and Roberta's sister during my interviews," Billy said smiling.

"Oh. Well, anyway, I thought I should tell her in person as soon as possible what had happened. Since I was there when Roberta died. I didn't want her to hear about it and wonder why I never thought to tell her. Her death doesn't change anything between me and Kate."

"That must have been a difficult conversation."

"She was shocked, naturally. After I told her what happened, she cried. Cried! Who in their right mind would cry for Roberta?"

"Your wife was close to her cousin?"

Matt sipped more beer and nodded. "Yeah. Kate really liked her. She said Roberta had always been nice to her. Probably the only person she was ever nice to, as far I know."

Billy made some quick notations. "Well, I'll leave you to get on with your evening, sir. I'm sorry to have disturbed your dinner hour."

Matt smiled weakly as he followed him to the door. "Let me know if you need any other information," he offered. "I'm happy to help."

"Thanks. I appreciate your cooperation." Billy sat in his vehicle and tapped his pencil on the steering wheel. He knew about Roberta's loan to Matt and was wondering if Roberta's death did in fact impact his marriage. After all, her death might have gotten him off the hook, and he might be hopeful that Kate would take him back. That could explain his rush to tell her that night. It was definitely an idea worth exploring.

CHAPTER 19

Billy asked Samantha to continue to act and plan events as she normally would under the sad circumstances. So, Samantha scheduled the remembrance luncheon for the Saturday after the viewing. Madeline was very curious to see *Roberta's natural habitat*, as she referred to it. Tom insisted on driving her since he knew the way, explaining that it was easy to get lost.

Madeline was surprised by how pretty Roberta's log house was. It was set near the lake, so there was plenty of sun. The front yard was a neat, lush lawn and the flower beds near the house had several white rhododendrons just beginning to shed their blooms as white peony buds were becoming visible. But she was astonished at the decor.

"Puppies and bunnies on decorative plates? The kind of sappy thing I could imagine Roberta making caustic remarks about. Don't tell me that her bedroom is decorated in fantastically feminine pink and white lace and floral chintz," Madeline said softly to Tom as they entered the living room.

"I assume you were expecting the Hansel and Gretel witch's house and oven?"

"At least a house in the dark, dark woods covered in thorny vines. But this may be worse."

The house was already full of the buzz of guests drinking, laughing and talking. The somber viewing was one thing, but a free lunch with alcohol was a totally different event. A bar had been set up on the kitchen pass-through. The long dining room table had ham, turkey, baked ziti, salad and bread next to plates and utensils. Since Samantha was busy talking to a young couple, they headed to the bar. Tony was pouring Fern a glass of wine as they approached.

"You really need to get a grip on yourself, Fern," Tony said.

Fern sniffled. "I know. But I just can't seem to stop crying," she whimpered.

"Look, here's Tom and his friend. Why don't you talk to them?" Tony smirked and winked at Tom as he walked away.

Fern looked startled and sniffled again.

"How are you doing, Fern? I imagine it is difficult." Madeline hoped she sounded sympathetic. Tom handed Madeline a drink and poured one for himself.

"Oh, sometimes I am fine. And then I think I should call Robbie to go out and eat or something, and then I remember she's really gone for good and I don't have a best friend anymore." Tears streamed down her face.

"I am so sorry, Fern. Good friends are hard to come by."

"Robbie always looked out for me. I didn't always appreciate it because she was so bossy. But now I miss her so much." She started to cry in earnest again. "Excuse me. I need to find a tissue."

Madeline glanced into the kitchen through the pass-through and was surprised to see Billy taking a pie out of the oven. She tapped Tom on the arm to draw his attention to him.

Tom chuckled. "Billy set himself up near the bar. A great spot for eavesdropping," he whispered to her.

Tom and Madeline moved toward Samantha and introduced themselves.

"Yes, I remember you from the viewing. Roberta said you two were new on the bus. She always kept me up to date on the commuter gossip and goings-on."

"Whether you wanted to know or not?" Tom smiled at her.

Samantha smiled back at him. "It really wasn't very interesting, but the bus people were a major part of her life."

"We are very sorry for your loss," Tom said. "You have a lovely home."

"Yes. It is really lovely. Did you decorate it yourself?" Madeline asked.

"Oh, my dear, yes. We enjoyed picking out furniture and decorative items. One of the few things we enjoyed doing together."

"Really? I had the impression you were very close." Madeline smiled sweetly as she lied.

"I would say close, but not really close. I think she was closer to Fern."

"Oh, poor Fern. She is so distraught. How will she ever eat their favorite salsa again without thinking about that party? And they put so much effort into making it just the way they liked it."

"I told Roberta she should just make her own from scratch, but she wasn't much of a cook. She would just cut up some jalapeños and habaneros to add to her favorite brand."

"Well, I don't know how she managed to do that at four in the morning. I am barely awake enough to get dressed, let alone cut up hot peppers!"

Samantha laughed. "No. She cut them up the night before and put the container in the fridge. Then, of course, she had to put a sticky note on the front door and the bathroom mirror to remind herself to take them!"

"That definitely makes more sense."

"Excuse me. I see some people I need to speak with. Thank you both for coming. It was nice to have met you," Samantha said as she walked away.

"You are good at getting the information we need," Tom said quietly. "I'm glad I picked you as my partner." He was standing very close to her, and Madeline felt her face grow warm.

She turned around quickly so Tom wouldn't see her blushing and almost bumped into Stephen. He had a plate piled high with food.

"Hello, Stephen," Tom said. "Did you bring your lovely wife?"

"No, Francesca was not interested in attending. She did not care much for Roberta."

"That is understandable. Did you know her well?"

Stephen looked puzzled. "Of course not. We had no contact other than on the bus. Oh, look! There are Moira and Joe. I must go say hello to them."

"I don't trust him. He's sly and evasive," Madeline commented once he was out of earshot.

"Rumors were all over town a couple of years ago about Roberta reporting him to the SEC and the police. It was right after he moved here. Story was he had advised her to buy stock in a company that went bankrupt right after she bought it. The rumors disappeared, and nothing seems to have come from her complaint."

"Well, it must have been nothing if he still has his job in the city. Whatever it may be. He is cagey about it."

Tom nodded. "I don't think he has anything to do with legal investments. My instinct tells me he's a con man."

"Really? Well, if he is and Roberta found out—"

"No. He's too smart. She would never be able to prove anything."

"So, you think he doesn't have a motive?"

Tom shrugged. "No more than anyone else Roberta trashed. If he is a con man, he is playing a long game, and Roberta was merely a petty annoyance. There was no reason for him to risk murder."

Jake and Tony were standing together by the fireplace, and Tom suggested they join them. As soon as they approached, the two men stopped their conversation.

"I'm surprised you two showed up," Tony said.

"Yes, well, we were on the bus when she died, so—" Madeline began.

"If I wasn't her neighbor, I wouldn't have bothered to come," Jake said.

"Oh, yes. I forgot. Do you live on this same street?" Madeline asked.

"Yeah, two houses down."

"Not nearly far enough away! Huh, Jake?" Tony offered.

"You don't live close by, yet you came, Tony," Tom said.

"Yeah, I'm here for the free booze and food. It's the least her sister could do, considering what a pain Roberta was to everyone."

"Yes, I suppose so," Madeline remarked. "Look at poor Matt. He looks like something the cat dragged in," she said gesturing in his direction.

He was a wrinkled mess slumped on the edge of the sofa with a haunted look on his face as he stared at Kate, who was across the room chatting with two other women.

"Yeah. Roberta ruined his life. But he was not smart about that loan. Should never have done that," Tony said.

Jake nodded. "I guess he had no choice, facing bankruptcy and all, you know. But maybe he shoulda gone bankrupt. I mean, at least he would have been his own man. You know, not under Roberta's thumb."

Tony chuckled. "And she had a mighty big thumb to be under."

Rosemary sidled over to them, looking beautiful in a simple black sheath, which complemented her tall, slender figure. Her long blond hair was pulled back into a French twist.

"So, do you two go everywhere together now?" Rosemary smiled at the group but spoke to Tom.

He smiled back. "No. But this is a bus-related event."

"Going on that principle means I should have brought Gunter. He always adds so much to a party," she quipped. "Actually, I am not sure if he is aware Roberta is deceased, let alone that she died on the bus."

The group stood in awkward silence for a few seconds. Madeline racked her brain for something to say. "Your wife isn't here, Tony?" she finally blurted out.

"Nah. She had to go to some luncheon with her mother and some other old ladies."

"Oh, too bad. I was hoping to meet her. There wasn't a chance at the viewing."

Madeline and Tom moved away and stood by a bookcase and surveyed the crowd. She turned to look at the photos on the shelf next to her. There in black and white were two young girls in pigtails, with broad smiles on their faces, each holding a giant pickle. "This must be Samantha and Roberta." She indicated the photo to Tom.

He leaned down to look at it closely and looked over the rest of the pictures. "This seems to be the only one of them together. All the later photos are individual or with other people."

"Makes you wonder how close they really were," Madeline said.

"Maybe."

Once back in the car, they sat in silence for several minutes.

"So. What do you think?" Tom asked.

"Well, we now know that Samantha had access to the pepper container," Madeline said. "And from the way Fern is acting, I just don't believe she killed Roberta."

"I agree. At least not on purpose."

"Samantha aside, I still think it was one of the bus people. Nobody else would have known the mechanics of the soiree or Roberta's habits."

"At the viewing, everybody was a local or a relative—I recognized most of them. But I also did check the book at the funeral parlor, and nobody unknown to us had signed it. There was nobody who looked out of place or on their own," Tom said.

"Nobody outside our group appeared in anyway curious to meet and talk to one of us at the viewing or today. I would think the killer would want to get a feel for what people were thinking. Is there suspicion she was murdered and if there's an active police investigation? The killer planned this so well, they would want to be certain that a problem wasn't heading their way."

"Or glory in their success," Tom added.

"Job well done and just step away. Could be the perfect crime!"

He shook his head. "No. I don't buy it. I think it is one of our bus suspects or Samantha. They either put the drugs in the food as it was passed around or doctored one of the containers."

Madeline looked sad as she stared out her window at Roberta's house. She was thinking that this adventure might not be a good idea after all. Her excitement about getting closer to Tom had blinded her to the reality that someone had been murdered. She was frightened. "Yes, I agree. But that leaves us no closer than when we started," she finally said softly.

"It may take time, but something will come up."

She nodded and continued to stare out of the window.

"Are you still comfortable with being involved in this investigation? You can opt out if you want to, you know," Tom said with a concerned look on his face.

"*Comfortable* may be too strong a word," she said and turned to look at him. She was astonished he had picked up on her feelings. "But I'm okay. However, I never nap on the bus any more. Unless you're there."

CHAPTER 20

The bold headline across the front page of the Wednesday edition of the *Cross Keys Bulletin* screamed BUS OF DEATH DRIVES MURDER VICTIM'S BODY INTO TOWN. Underneath was added *Commuter Killer Confuses Cops*.

"Maddie! Did you know about this?" Jeff yelled in excitement over the phone. "The entire town is in an uproar."

"Uh. Well. Yes. But Tom swore me to secrecy. Sorry."

"Tom! It appears you have been keeping more than one secret from us, young lady. You are coming over for dinner tonight and spilling it all. I will make your favorite lasagna. See you as soon as you get off the *Bus of Death*."

The entire clique was on the bus the day the news came out. "My heavens! This is disturbing news!" Moira looked alarmed and a little pale. "How in the world did this happen?" she asked addressing the group.

Fern started sobbing yet again, and Brian patted her on the arm. He had moved seats permanently to Roberta's old one.

"This has to be some kind of mistake," Tony said. "I bet there was a mix-up at the lab. We were all there. Nobody poisoned her. We all ate the same food. Right, guys?"

"Yeah. How would the poison get into the food? You know, I bought my cheese and crackers at a store in the city, so it wasn't in my contribution," Jake said.

"I made the guacamole at home, but everybody ate some, including me." Matt sounded defensive.

"My homemade nachos certainly didn't make anyone sick. Let alone kill anybody," Moira huffed.

The group fell silent again as they thought about this.

"It's just another example of how incompetent the local police are," Moira continued. "The idea of one of us being a killer is ludicrous."

"But the article said it was based on the autopsy report," Jake said.

"Most likely it is some misinformation fed to a gullible reporter," said Stephen. "After all, the only individuals who added anything to the food were Roberta herself and Fern. It seems unlikely either of them added the deadly drugs."

Fern was now too upset to even cry. She stared wide-eyed at the group. "I brought the salsa. Sassy Salsa. *Extra Spicy, Sizzling Hot! Hot! Hot!* It says so on the label. There's a picture on it of a pretty woman breathing fire. It was Robbie's favorite brand. But it wasn't hot enough for her, so she always added peppers to it. I put in some extra garlic, salt and other spices because the extra peppers overwhelmed everything else. That's the way we always ate it." She looked imploringly around the group.

The regulars looked at each other and then whispered in pairs. Madeline thought they even seemed to look suspiciously at each other.

The group finally fell silent for the rest of the trip, but Madeline noticed that nobody fell asleep as usual.

* * *

Madeline had called Tom to tell him about Jeff's call, and he suggested she bring Harry and Jeff by the bar after dinner. He was acquainted with them and thought he might be able to help smooth things over and answer questions.

As soon as Madeline arrived at their house, they gave her a large glass of wine and then demanded answers.

"Well, there is still really nothing to tell. She was poisoned. It isn't like there was a large knife sticking out of her back with blood dripping everywhere, the murderer standing over her with a scary grimace on their face. Her death still happened the way I described it. She was found dead in her seat."

"So, who do you think did it?" Harry asked.

"Uh, we don't know yet."

"We?" Jeff insinuated.

"Tom and I are, unofficially, trying to figure it out. We have a list of likely suspects but...we haven't really gotten very far in the investigation," she said sheepishly. She realized it had to appear to them that she was tagging along after Tom like a pop star's fan. "He suggested I bring you two over to the bar later to talk about it."

"Great! We get to see you two together. Body language never lies. Did Tom ask you to help, or did you volunteer?" Jeff asked.

"He asked me."

"And where do you meet to discuss your ideas?" Harry asked.

"His office at The Opossum."

"Ha! I told you so. You owe me a Chez Pierre dinner!" Jeff whooped. "I knew there was something going on."

"Nothing is going on! We are simply working together."

Madeline refused to tell them the list of suspects, which led to a guessing game in which they concluded that Martha, the bus driver, had done it, since she most resembled a butler in this story.

"Glad you guys came over," Tom greeted them with a broad smile. He sent them to a table by the fireplace after he took their drink orders.

"Well, isn't that a fancy green drink Maddie has?" Jeff commented.

"Yes. *Maddie* suggested there was a need for a special Opossum cocktail. So, I am experimenting with different combinations of alcohol and color."

"I see," Jeff said and smiled at Madeline.

"I think it is a good suggestion." Tom smiled warmly at Madeline as he sat down next to her. Harry and Jeff exchanged knowing glances.

"Harry and Jeff tell me that the town is abuzz with gossip about Roberta's murder. You know, on the *Bus of Death*."

Tom laughed. "Yeah, I know. I hear everybody sitting at the bar talking about it. It actually has been the Bus of Death as far as my back is concerned. It is a bumpy ride."

"So, Tom," Harry started, "Maddie says you two have a theory about who the murderer is."

"Actually, I said we have a list of suspects. But I didn't give you any specifics," Madeline interrupted, glancing at Tom.

"No, she didn't. Maddie says it is creepy riding on the bus with a killer," Jeff said.

"She is right. But I don't think she is in danger," Tom said.

"So, I guess you two are working closely together on this," Jeff suggested.

"Yes, we are. And it has been a pleasure to spend time with Maddie. She has been a great help also."

Jeff nudged Harry's foot under the table. "Well, after you solve it—and I am sure you will—we will have you both over for dinner so you can give us all the juicy details," Harry said.

"I look forward to it," Tom said. Madeline finished her drink in one gulp.

On the Thursday afternoon bus, Tom asked Madeline if she could come to The Opossum on Saturday. "Moira and her Joey will be there," he explained.

"How on earth did you manage that?"

"I found an opportunity to mention to Joe that I just got a bottle of his favorite port. It's expensive and hard to find. He jumped at the chance to stop by. Moira approved."

"So, you can talk to him, and I can talk to Moira." Tom nodded. "You know, every time she calls him *my Joey*, I think of a baby kangaroo."

Tom laughed. "I never looked at it that way. But Joe is like a kangaroo, he hops to all of Moira's commands."

CHAPTER 21

Madeline entered The Opossum a little after six to find Moira and Joey already sitting at the bar talking to Tom. She greeted them and joined the group, sitting on a stool next to Moira.

"Can I get you a Opossumtini?"

Madeline smiled. "Absolutely."

Tom placed a martini glass in front of her. The drink was the color of Windex and had tiny marshmallows floating in it.

"Okay. It's different. I like the color. Nice of you to try so hard." She took a sip and nodded in approval. "Not bad."

"We were just discussing Roberta's death," Tom informed Madeline.

Moira nodded. "Naturally, we were all devastated by her death. But now it is even worse to know somebody we sit in close quarters with for hours a week may have killed her. My Joey has been beside himself. He just worries about me so much. Right, sweetie?" Moira said as she sipped a vodka gimlet. From what Madeline could see, Joey was not feeling any anxiety about it.

"Yes, dear," he said as if on automatic pilot and went back to his port and chatting with Tom.

"Fern is even more upset now. She must feel lonely and frightened," Madeline observed.

"Aren't we all? Anyway, it's her own fault if she's alone. Roberta always said that Fern was an oversexed bimbo. Always chasing the wrong man for the wrong reasons," Moira confided.

"What a terrible thing to say about your best friend."

"Yes. But she was always looking out for Fern. Trying, without much luck, to keep her on the straight and narrow. When Fern's second marriage went on the rocks, it was Roberta that helped her find a job and made her think about having a real career and going back to school."

"That makes Roberta sound like a true friend. She really helped Fern."

Moira looked thoughtful. "Roberta micromanaged her life, especially her love life. It was sad the way she criticized her about it."

"Did Fern listen to her?"

"Not really, no. Every one of Fern's affairs fizzled out. Bad choices. Even married men. Hoping she'd steal them away from their wives. You know the type."

Madeline sipped her drink and didn't respond. "I am a little surprised. She seems so sweet. Did she ever go after any of the men in town?"

"Oh, my goodness, she flirts with them all the time. She keeps Brian and Jake strung along, thinking that they have a chance. Roberta used to make fun of them. *Dogs with their tongues hanging out* I think she said once."

"That's bad. But sounds like our Roberta, all right."

"Yes, indeed. Fern isn't the smartest girl, and so Roberta took care of her as much as possible. I must admit I was a little surprised by the extent of her wailing. Fern is very much into herself—she's one of those new-age types. You know what I mean. She's into her own feelings and trying to *heal* herself with crystals, auras, herbs and amulets. I mean, I would think that she would be cured by now if that stuff worked." Moira rechecked her hair. "She is always trying to look innocent and helpless. It might work on the men she meets, but believe me, she's really anything but."

Moira lowered her voice, leaned closer and placed her hand gently on Madeline's arm. "I have a feeling Fern's got someone to comfort her, if you know what I mean."

"Really?"

Moira took another sip of her drink. "And Roberta didn't approve. She counseled her to never expect anything from men except trouble."

"Sounds like Roberta didn't like men or marriage much."

"From what I know, years ago, Roberta had one great love. He was a local man who lived in Lyon, separated from his wife. Roberta fully expected, after their lengthy affair, he'd marry her when his divorce was final. But it never happened. He reconciled with his wife and ended it. After that, she soured on romance and never tried again."

"That is sad."

They sat in silence for a few seconds. While she sipped her blue drink, Madeline was trying unsuccessfully to imagine anyone being in love with Roberta.

"Yes. And over the years she just became more bitter. All she had was her sister, her job and Fern."

"What was Roberta's job?"

"She worked in the complaint department of Global Insurance. She handled complaints from all over the world."

"What a perfect occupation for her."

"I never thought of that. She could certainly dish out the complaints, so I guess she knew how to deal with them from others," Moira said and laughed and rechecked her hair. "Roberta and I got along, although she did not like many people, and she hated pretentiousness. That's why she never liked Stephen." Joey quietly urged Tom to top up Moira's cocktail. He did so as Moira's attention was focused on Madeline.

She leaned close to Madeline. "You know, Stephen is a major mover and shaker. He makes bundles of money. Once he gave us an insider stock tip. He said it was risky, but that he had put twenty thousand dollars into it. So, Roberta put five thousand dollars of her savings into the stock. My Joey said that speculating on a stock like that was simply gambling, so we didn't buy any. The stock went straight up, and Roberta was crowing about all the money she was making and what she was going to do with it. But then the company was found to be lying about something important concerning its products. The stock tanked. Roberta lost all her money and blamed Stephen. She said she would fix him. She reported him to all the proper authorities. He nearly got in serious trouble."

"Roberta certainly seemed to enjoy tormenting people."

"Yes. Lord knows she was the mistress of pain on that bus."

"Speaking of pain, is there any way to lower Jake's voice?"

Moira shook her head. "He is so uncouth. He's a manual laborer." She waved her hands in a dismissive gesture. "No prospects of being anything interesting or successful. He's Tony's friend, and that's the most you can say about him, and that is not saying much. He and Roberta had some kind of running feud going. Something to do with their community-road maintenance. I never paid any attention. I don't like to gossip. She even started a rumor that he plays for the other team." Moira looked knowingly at Madeline, who nodded in acknowledgment and sipped her drink.

"What about Tony? Did he have a problem with Roberta?"

Moira looked thoughtful and wagged a red-tipped forefinger at Madeline. "You're very nosy, aren't you?"

"Just trying to get to know people. It's hard when you're new, you know."

Moira looked sympathetic as she sipped her drink. "Well, it is common knowledge that Tony has—shall we say—an eye for the ladies. After all, he is extremely handsome. His wife is from an incredibly influential family in Cross Keys. Yes, indeed, he married very well. His family was not a good one, to put it mildly. Tony is just plain lucky he's so handsome, or he would be working at the Pit or worse. His wife, Olivia, is a lovely girl. Beautiful, as you saw, but also smart, sweet and always beautifully dressed and groomed."

"Yes. I saw her at the viewing. She didn't seem very friendly."

"Olivia is used to associating with only the best kind of people. Naturally, she finds certain people beneath her notice. Her parents were not happy about the marriage, but rumor had it that Olivia was pregnant, so they went along with what she wanted. They had a huge wedding in church, and she wore white." Moira raised her eyebrows in disapproval. "And they bought them the most beautiful house as a wedding present. But there was never a baby. So, I don't know if she really was pregnant or had a miscarriage or what the true story was."

"So, Roberta believed Tony was fooling around on the side. That's why she made all those comments about him. If it's true, it would be awkward."

"Awkward! Oh, you better believe that he is scared to death of any infidelity being discovered. Certainly, the house is not in Tony's name, and he owes his job to Olivia's father, so he would probably have to move into the mobile home with his trashy mother and sister." Moira laughed and jingled her bangles. "Oh, yes, Tony would be kicked off the gravy train big time."

"Roberta didn't seem to fight with Brian."

"Brian is sweet and totally harmless. You know, I don't think he has a mean bone in his body—or a brain in his head. Lord knows how he makes a living. He just floats along with the breeze collecting every lost dog and cat he finds."

"He does seem like a free spirit."

"I even think he is kinda cute! You know, in a sad-puppy-dog sort of way. It's those blond curls hanging out from under his hat, I guess. I just wish he would take that filthy old cap off. But he was very wary of Roberta. Brian doesn't like confrontation. But it is obvious that he is sweet on Fern, and I am sure that Roberta didn't approve."

"But why not? He's a nice guy, and he isn't married."

"Roberta didn't want Fern to settle for just anyone, you know."

"Well, how many real options does Fern have? I mean the woods of Pennsylvania aren't exactly crawling with eligible bachelors. Are they?"

Moira shrugged. "Well, I wouldn't know dear, I never go into the woods. It's full of bugs and snakes." Moira sipped more of her bottomless gimlet, and Madeline finished off her drink.

"Alice seems a little odd," Madeline said to change the subject.

"*Odd* doesn't quite cover it, dear! She looks meek as a mouse but can be mean as snake. None of us like her. Roberta found her and plopped her down in the seat across from her. Probably to aggravate Brian and to annoy everybody else. And she smells. Probably all those cats she keeps."

"Really? She seems very meek and mild. I haven't seen mean."

"Once Elizabeth made an offhand comment about how she hates cats. Well, let me tell you, Alice went ballistic. The foul words that came out of her mouth would make any normal person blush. And she wouldn't let it go. She kept harassing Elizabeth and calling her insulting names. Roberta thought it was all very funny."

"Did she threaten Elizabeth?"

"No. Just spit out venom. She eventually stopped. I guess she finally ran out of insulting terms."

"How are you ladies doing? Can I refresh your drinks?" Tom asked them with a large smile and a cocktail shaker in his hand.

Without waiting for an answer, he placed a coupette glass in front of Madeline and poured a violet-colored liquid into it and garnished it with a twist of lemon.

Madeline gave him a questioning look. "Another iteration of the Opossumtini? My, my, you have been busy, haven't you?"

"Yes. I told you I was working on it."

"My, what a pretty drink!" Moira exclaimed.

"Isn't it, though? Try one," Madeline suggested as she took a small sip and nodded in approval.

"No, thank you. I think my Joey has had enough bar time. Let's go get a table and have dinner, dear." Joey looked forlornly at the bottle of port sitting in front of him but dutifully helped Moira off the barstool, thanked Tom and headed off. "See you both on Monday," she trilled as Joey helped her to the table.

Tom turned to Madeline. "You two seemed cozy. Anything interesting?"

"Tons, but not much insight. Let's say Tony and Jake had reasons to dislike Roberta, but I don't know about murder."

Tom nodded. "More grist for the mill. You hungry?"

"I thought you would never ask. Oh, I vote for the lavender Opossumtini."

CHAPTER 22

Moira and Joe lived right in town in a large two-story house with a generous front porch, featuring an old-fashioned porch swing and love seat glider. Billy mounted the steps and rang the bell. Joe opened the door almost immediately. He was wearing a work apron and holding a caddy full of cleaning supplies.

"Sorry to bother you, Joe, but I need to speak to you without Moira around. I assume she is in the city since this is a work day."

"Yes. Peace will reign for another five hours at least," Joe said and laughed. "Come on in. And since Moira isn't home, I will let you keep your shoes on."

Billy carefully wiped his feet on the doormat and stepped into the entrance.

"Want some coffee?" Joe asked.

"That would be nice. Thanks."

"So, what can I do for you?" Joe asked once they were settled at the round wooden kitchen table.

"Well…um…this is a bit awkward. But I need to know. Did you bet with Bart Grickly?"

Joe's mouth popped open in surprise. "Uh…yes…yes, I did bet with him from time to time. How did you find out?"

"Oh, just solid police work." *Henpecked* has to be Joe, he thought to himself. "Did you happen to see him the day he died?"

"No. Last I saw him was at the gym a couple of days before that. I only bet occasionally. You know, when I thought I had a good tip or hunch. Moira doesn't approve of gambling. Obviously, I didn't want her to find out, so I always met him in Port Potter."

"Do you happen to know anybody else who bet with him? Did you ever run into any other clients when you saw him?"

"Billy, he didn't exactly host mixers for his clients."

The chief laughed and nodded.

"How did you find Grickly to begin with?"

"I go to The Gym in Port Potter." Joe smiled at the look on Billy's face. "I know. It doesn't look like it does me any good. I admit I don't work very hard, but it is a good way to get away from Moira for a while on weekends, if she's nagging me too much. She wouldn't be caught dead in a gym. Anyway, I got friendly with some of the guys, and one of them turned out to be Bart."

"Do you think they were his clients too?"

Joe shrugged. "Might be. They certainly are sports fans. It was the main topic of conversation. That and women."

"If I go to the gym with you, could you point them out to me?"

"Sure."

"Great. Give me a call when you're going next, and I will join you."

"How's this Saturday around eleven? Moira is usually back from the beauty parlor by then with a list of chores for me to do."

"Sounds good. Thanks again. And I will let myself out."

"Oh, Billy—please don't tell anyone about my gambling. If Moira found out, there'd be hell to pay."

"Your secret is safe with me. See you Saturday."

* * *

As arranged, Billy met Joe at The Gym in Port Potter. Set just off the interstate in a mini mall, it featured weight machines, free weights, treadmills, stationary bikes and ellipticals, plus classes in yoga, Pilates, boxing and spinning in the early mornings and evenings and on weekends. The Gym was owned and operated by Rachel Taylor, a former professional body builder.

After a short conversation with the perky young woman at the reception desk and a much longer conversation with Rachel, he found Joe with four young men in the free-weights area. He had barely escaped joining after Rachel's persistent sales pitch, but he did receive a pass for a free personal training session with Rachel.

Billy surveyed the group but did not recognize any of the young men.

"Hi, Billy," Joe said as he finished his bicep curls. "Hey, guys. This is Chief West from Cross Keys. He is trying to find out who killed Bart." The four young men looked a little nervous.

"Chief, this is Zach Hitchins, Ricky Turner, Mike Nowak and Trey Williams." Joe pointed at each in turn. Zach was overweight, with hair down to his shoulders and a beard down to the middle of his chest; Ricky was thin and buff, with a man bun and neatly trimmed beard; Mike was very tall and slim, with a crew cut and a handlebar moustache; and Trey looked like a serious body builder, with bulging legs and arms.

Billy nodded at the group. "You were all friends with Bart?" They nodded. "How long had you known him?"

"I knew him my whole life," Zach said. "We were in school together."

"I just know him from the gym," said Trey.

"Me and Mike went to high school with him too," Ricky offered.

"So, three of you knew him well. Do you know of anybody who had a serious grudge against him? Any client or friend he had a dispute with?"

They looked at each other and shrugged. "Joelle wasn't happy that Bart was seeing Rachel on the side. She could get pretty pissed off. She stabbed him a year ago when she found out he was cheating on her," Mike said. "But they worked it out, I guess."

Joelle never mentioned Bart's cheating, Billy thought.

"Bart never mentioned being threatened?"

"Bart never talked about his business with us," Zach said.

"Never?"

"Not much, anyway."

"He had a big business to run. A large distribution network from what I know. It must have kept him very busy," Billy suggested.

Zach shrugged. "Yeah. He was smart. He got other people to do the drudge work for him."

"What do you mean?"

"He ran part of his drug business on a consignment basis."

"So, how did that work?"

Zach looked at the other guys and shrugged his shoulders. "Bart would supply the product and the the seller got paid a commission, I guess you'd call it. A percent of what was sold. Saved him a lot of time and he sold a lot of product."

"What if the seller tried to cheat him?"

Zach snickered. "Yeah, that didn't happen very often. Bart was brutal with his punishment to anybody who tried to cross him."

"Did any of you see him the day he died?"

They looked at each other and then as a group shook their heads.

"Are you certain?" He looked hard at Zach and Ricky as he recalled his interview with Agatha.

They looked around at each other again. "Now that I think about it, I think we were at the Tickity that night," Zach said, and Ricky nodded his head in agreement.

"Did Bart have an argument with anybody?"

"Just a few words with some bitchy old lady."

"Nobody else?"

"Not that I saw," Ricky said and Zach nodded in agreement.

"Did he say he was going to come back later and meet somebody?"

"Don't know," Zach said. "I know he took Joelle home. She was really out of it. I don't know why he would come back later."

"Well, he obviously did come back, and it must have been important. Look, I'm trying to solve the murder of your friend. Do any of you have any idea who killed him?"

"Sorry. We don't know anything," Mike said, and they all turned back to the weights.

Billy's gut told him Zach and Ricky knew more than they were saying. He took their names and contact information and gave them his business card. "Thanks for your help. If you think of anything else, give me a call."

They nodded and went back to their workout.

Joe walked him out. "Nice guys, right?"

"Yeah. Thanks for the introductions. Have a good workout."

CHAPTER 23

"Come on, Wally! Pick me the big winner. I really need it!" Matt was almost yelling, and he looked away for a few seconds, rubbing his forehead as though he had a headache. "Seriously, I really need it, you know," he said in a calmer voice. Matt was standing in front of the counter looking hopefully at the rows of colorful lottery tickets. "It's Saturday, so the draw for the big one is tonight."

Walter Bolter was one of those people who never seemed to age. He had looked old his entire adult life, and at this point he could be either an old fifty or a young eighty or anywhere in between. He had owned Bolter's as long as anybody could remember. It was an old-fashioned newspaper and candy store. The bell on the door tinkled as people entered, and the wooden floorboards creaked as they walked across them. The aromas of wood, tobacco, bubblegum and newsprint blended together with a faint, underlying musty scent. The shelves and display cases were antiques made of glass and polished wood.

"Matt, you shouldn't waste your money on this junk," Wally said gently. "I only sell them 'cause I have to, what with the competition and all. I mean, the odds of you winning are a zillion to one. It even says so on the back of the ticket."

"Some people get lucky, you know!"

Wally shook his head. "I hope you win. I really do."

Matt took his tickets and carefully put them in his pocket. The doorbell tinkled as Tom entered the store. He picked up a copy of the Bulletin and put a dollar on the counter.

"Hi guys. How's it going?"

"Can't complain," Wally said.

"Been better," Matt mumbled.

Tom could see perfectly well that Matt was not doing well. His clothes were wrinkled and stained, he was unshaven, and his hair had spots of gray that had not been there a few weeks ago.

"Crazy news about Roberta," Tom said.

"I never liked the woman. Never had a nice word to say," Wally said.

"No loss in my book. As you both know," Matt added.

"Everybody had problems with Roberta," Tom pointed out.

"Easy for you to say," Matt snapped at Tom.

Tom shrugged. "I guess you're right about that. You got the brunt of it from her."

"Yeah. I've been stupid, and I have made mistakes. Now at least I don't have to hear from her every day on that damn bus."

Tom smiled at him. "I hear you. Matt, you are talking to some-one who has made more stupid mistakes than you can even imagine."

"Maybe. But borrowing money from Roberta wasn't one of them. And as if I don't have enough to worry about, Billy obviously thinks I had a good motive to kill her. He's right. I did. He asked me about the bottle of Tabasco I gave her as if it contained the drugs. It was brand-new, in the box, with all the crap they put over the lid so nobody can poison it. In fact, Roberta complained about it being so difficult to open. I wish I had seen something! I wish I knew what had happened! All I remember of that day is her yelling at me in line, eating on the bus, and then Moira finding her dead."

"Why was Roberta yelling at you in line?"

"I walked off with her precious Harrods bag. She gave it to me to hold for her while she went to the ladies' room, and then I dis-covered that I had lost my lighter, so I went to get one. There was a young woman in front of me buying, like, five fashion and gossip magazines and arguing with the clerk about the total. It took longer than it should have, and when I got back Roberta was hopping mad."

"You didn't look in the bag?"

"No. I could see plastic and paper party stuff sticking out, you know, plates, napkins, forks. But I didn't dig around in it. Why would I? I know what you are thinking. Her pepper container was in it. How would I know that I would be given the opportunity to put poison in her pepper container? I didn't know she had the peppers in her bag." He sighed in frustration. "If wishing somebody dead would work, she would have died several times over from my thoughts. But I couldn't kill anybody, not even her. Even I am not that stupid."

Tom nodded. "Hang in there. Things will get better."

"I hope so."

"Stop by the bar sometime. I'll buy you a drink."

"Thanks. I may take you up on that."

* * *

Tom was way behind on his spring yard and garden work. The commuting meant his weekdays were useless, and the weekends, with the bar to attend to, were busy as well. The season was moving on fast, and it was obvious he couldn't wait any longer. The Cascade Garden Center was his preferred place to buy his mulch, lime, herbicides, fertilizer and annual plants. It was located west of town by a few miles. He was looking at the petunias and impatiens, when he ran into Jake.

"I see we think alike," Tom said. "I am behind this year. I don't know how you do anything around the house and yard when you are commuting."

Jake nodded. "You know, it's tough. That's why I always look for time-savers, like the preplanted containers they have here. It's a little more expensive but worth it."

Tom agreed, and they walked around together commenting on the various plants.

"My big problem is deer. They eat everything," Jake said.

"Yes, they certainly are a problem. I put in a deer fence. It works really well. I was thinking of getting another dog, and I figured I could keep the dog in and the deer out."

"What kind of dog?"

Tom smiled. "Not sure. I will probably look for a rescue. I've had good luck with them in the past."

"I like dogs. Never got one because of Roberta. She hated dogs. She complained about every dog in the development. She reported a toy poodle to animal control as a vicious attack dog. The poor old lady who owned it nearly lost her mind when they took it away. She got it back eventually. I had enough problems with Roberta as it was."

"She knew how to make friends, didn't she?"

"Right. She made my life hell."

"I think I heard about that. Something about some problems in the development."

"Yeah. The treasurer of the board of directors wanted the contract for snow removal and road maintenance for the community to go to his wife's brother. He twisted arms on the board, you know. The other contractor's bid was lower, and one honest board member filed suit to remove the treasurer. My cousin works for the lawyer who handled it and told me all about it. The treasurer's brother-in-law lost the contract after the investigation and the treasurer lost his position."

"So what did it have to do with Roberta?"

"Roberta was a good friend of the treasurer. Figures, right? She thought I had something to do with it because of my cousin. Roberta made it personal. She started, you know, making shit up about me and my business. At the time, I was building a contracting business here so I could quit commuting. She spread her lies all over social media and by word of mouth. It got bad."

"How bad?"

"I lost customers. I had to file suit for libel. She finally backed off, but it cost me time and money. My business is still recovering. The woman was not sane. I steered clear of her, except for the bus. Now that she's gone, maybe I've got a chance."

"She certainly seems to have been happy when she was making others miserable. Like Matt," Tom said, prompting him.

"Yeah, she really liked to push his buttons. You know, the day she died she had been yelling at him nonstop when we were getting on the bus."

"About what?"

"Who knows? She didn't need a reason. She lit into him like she was going to eat him alive. Something about her green bag. I just tuned her out."

Tom nodded in agreement as he picked up a day lily. "She was horrible. Still, nobody should die like that."

"That's true. Well, I'm headed over to the roses."

"Nice to see you. Good luck with the deer."

"Thanks. You too"

Nice guy, Tom thought. He mentally checked him off the suspect list.

CHAPTER 24

On Saturdays, Madeline would occasionally take the time to explore some of the more out-of-the-way shops. Halfway to Walmart from Cross Keys, a small strip of stores sat beside the three-lane road. Here you could buy a reptile at The Reptilian, get a tattoo at the Ink Spot Fine Art and Tattoo Emporium, shop for organic foods and supplements at Mother Knows Best, or get in touch with your spiritual side at the Feast of the Spirit.

Madeline found the latter inexplicably fascinating. The store was an artfully staged, calm, comforting environment. Incense was constantly burning with chants or soundscape music softly playing in the background. While it focused on the occult and new-age products, there were also an extensive section of healing herbs, grown behind the store, some half-decent costume jewelry and a proprietary anti-aging face-and-eye cream that she found effective.

The owner was a woman named Sara Beth. Tall and thin, she dressed in flowing, gauzy fabrics and Birkenstock sandals. Many layers of varying lengths of beads and amulets hung from her neck and wrists. Her hair was long, unnaturally blond and worn either flowing free or in a single braid. Either the meditation and face creams worked to keep her looking young or she had undergone plastic surgery. In any case, Madeline suspected she was older than she appeared.

During store hours, Sara Beth would sit at an elaborate loom, supposedly weaving a complex pattern. However, whenever a customer came in, she would leave her work and follow them around to sell them items or suggest a tarot-card reading. The weaving never appeared to progress, and Madeline suspected it was just for show.

This Saturday, as she was looking around the store, Fern came in. They exchanged a smile and a nod of recognition. Fern still looked very sad with puffy eyes and a red nose.

"How are you, Fern?" Madeline asked.

"Oh, you know, I'm doing okay, I guess." She took a deep sigh. "I decided I needed to get out, and Sara Beth has been so helpful and understanding."

"Yes, the store is really nice. Do you come here often?"

"As much as I can. It's a comforting place for me."

Sara Beth walked over to Fern and put her arm around her. "How are you today, dear?" she said with a concerned look.

"I feel better today, you know, more centered." Fern gave her a half-hearted smile.

"Oh, my dear, the loss of your close friend, under such awful circumstances and leaving a cloud of suspicion over your group of friends, is very traumatizing to your whole aura." The proprietor circled her hands in the air as if pushing the aura around.

Fern sighed deeply again. "I miss her so much. What should I do, Sara Beth?"

The woman looked pensive. "You need to concentrate on the positives in your life, dear. You have your health and your beauty. Keep meditating and journaling, of course. Getting all those intense emotions on paper will help you sort out your feelings and find your direction. Speaking of positives—"

"Oh, it is magical, just as you predicted!" Fern's entire face lit up with a smile. "We are still so much in love. We meet when we can and talk about everything. I wish he could be with me more. Especially now, when I feel so lost." Fern shrugged her shoulders. "But I know we are meant to be together, and I need to be patient and trust in our love."

Madeline could not believe what she was hearing. She wondered how Roberta had felt about her affair or if she had known about it. She moved on to a display of crystals and pretended to be interested in them while she continued to eavesdrop.

"Those crystals are not only beautiful, they are powerful," Sara Beth called out. "And they're on sale. Twenty-five percent off for a limited time only. And all the herbs are BOGO today."

"BOGO?" Madeline asked.

"*Buy one get one free.*" Sara Beth beamed at her.

Madeline nodded.

The shop owner took Fern's hand. "Remember, I warned you to be careful of this man," she said. "Remember what we learned from our last reading. Passion can blind you. Keep you from seeing reality. You need to get some clarity."

Fern looked thoughtful. "I know. I've been giving a lot of thought to the drumming idea that you suggested the last time I was in here."

"Yes, that would be so healing for you, dear. Perfect to help you through this difficult period in your life. It gives you such a physical feeling of oneness with the universe, in addition to the spiritual well-being. You feel physically transported." Sara Beth beamed at the younger woman. "It is an ancient practice. Of course, you know that the Druids used drumming at Stonehenge."

"Oh, that sounds so...spiritual. Do I need a Druid too?"

Sara Beth looked stupefied but continued. "The sound of the drums was amplified by the stones and created a soothing, trancelike state. And you're in luck. I saved the best drum for you." Sara Beth smiled and spread her arms wide. "I just knew you would be back for it."

"Oh, thank you. Thank you so much! I guess that I better buy it, then. Oh, and you left me a message that my unicorn journal has finally arrived."

Sara Beth closed her eyes and took a deep, cleansing breath. "I am so glad that you reminded me. Yes, the journal is in, and it is quite a lovely book."

Fern smiled brightly. "Oh, thank you, Sara Beth! Thank you so much! What would I ever do without you? Especially now that Robbie is gone."

"Not *gone*, dear. Transformed and transported. Her energy still surrounds you."

Madeline could not stomach listening to this conversation any longer and decided that now was a good time to leave, before Roberta's energy could surround her also. She started walking toward the door.

"Please stop by again," Sara Beth called out. "We get new items in nearly every week. And we have pop-up sales every day also."

"Thanks. I will," Madeline said. "Bye, Fern. See you Monday."

Fern waved. "Yes, see you then."

Madeline wondered about Fern's affair. Was he married? Did he live nearby? Had Roberta known about him? Apparently, Fern did have secrets to protect.

"So, you are acquainted with that woman who just left? She comes in from time to time. I sense a great deal of anxiousness in her."

"Oh, she's a new commuter on the bus. Her name is Madeline something. I don't know her very well, really. Her husband ran off with a younger woman. She is throwing herself at Tom Firemark. You must know him. He owns The Opossum. Tall, good-looking—"

"Oh, yes. I know who he is," Sara Beth nodded knowingly. Over the years, she had had many customers who were interested in him. She smiled and patted Fern's arm. She would store that little tidbit of information away until the next time Madeline came in.

CHAPTER 25

Tom was pleased to find Ralph still had his internet-based criminal background accounts up to date. PIs were able to use them to garner information about cheating spouses, scam artists and other targets of their investigations. It would come in handy to check if any of the suspects had a history of problems with the law, the IRS or the DMV.

Jake was a solid citizen. Nothing came up on him, not even a parking ticket. But Tom did find out that he had been married and that his ex-wife had sued for divorce on grounds of adultery. She had claimed he was having an affair with another man. Tom wondered if this was something Roberta had found out about and was using against him. But he wasn't sure Jake would care. And, of course, it might not be true. Divorces could get extremely ugly.

Tony on the other hand had many issues. He had numerous speeding tickets in different states and an arrest for drunk and disorderly in Port Potter just a few years ago, and Tom knew he had hung around with an unsavory crowd before he married Olivia and his father-in-law forced him to clean up his act. Maybe he had not really given up all his old friends and habits. It was obvious Tony had a lot to lose, so if Roberta had some incriminating information on him and was threatening him with it, it was a great motive.

He found nothing on Samantha or Fern. Matt had some problems with credit but other than that had no issues.

But he found something interesting on Alice. Her husband was in an accident a year ago and was currently on disability. But he had filed a claim with his insurance company, which was denied. His company was Global Insurance, the same place Roberta worked in the complaint department. Perhaps there was a connection there. He wouldn't put it past Roberta to screw up his claim out of pure meanness. In addition, the Millers were in trouble with the IRS for unpaid back taxes.

* * *

The next Monday afternoon, Madeline plucked up her courage and asked Alice if she could sit next to her, since Brian's old seat was now available.

"It's empty, so suit yourself," Alice replied.

"Thanks." Madeline stored her bag in the overhead bin and sat down. She had expected to have to work hard to get Alice to speak to her. "How long have you been commuting?" Madeline began.

"I've been on the bus for approximately thirteen months, five days and one and a half hours."

"Well, I've only been riding for a few months full-time."

"Yes, I noticed."

"I love living in Cross Keys but didn't want to give up my job in the city."

"Most of us are in the same boat. No jobs in Cross Keys can compete with Manhattan in terms of pay."

"Everyone on the bus seems to be friends." Madeline was struggling to think of things to say.

"Not really."

"Well, you all have parties."

Alice smirked. "That was Roberta's idea. She loved to eat, especially when others paid."

"Did you know Roberta well?" Alice looked as though Madeline had slapped her in the face.

"No! She was a coarse, vindictive and unpleasant person."

Madeline noticed that her seatmate sat with her feet flat on the floor, the palms of both hands resting on her thighs, and she seemed to be constantly smoothing out her wrinkle-free skirt, which was covered with pet hair.

"Her death was shocking, though, wasn't it?"

"Not really."

"Oh? Why do you say that?"

"She was not a good person. She was mean, and nobody liked her. She deserved what she got."

"She deserved to be murdered?"

"Why do you care? Was she ever nice to you? Did you even know her?"

"No, but generally speaking, murder is not a normal way to die. And I was here when it happened. You were sitting right across from her. Doesn't it concern you? You could have been poisoned, you know. It's frightening."

Alice sighed and looked away from Madeline out the bus window across the aisle. "I was shocked, naturally. But I can't say that I miss having her around."

"What made you start commuting?"

She smoothed her skirt and shook her head. "Like everybody else, I need a good-paying job. My husband was in a bad accident at home, and the insurance didn't cover all of it, and everything was very expensive."

"Who was your insurer?"

"Global Insurance."

Of course, Roberta's company, thought Madeline. "Aren't they awful, these insurance companies? You pay year after year, and then when you need to make a claim, they won't pay, for some obscure reason."

"That is so true!"

"Did you complain?"

"Heavens, yes! I complained and complained. I wrote letters, I called, but to no avail."

"They always come up with some technicality that no reasonable person would think of."

"Oh, you are so right." She smoothed her skirt again. "Well, they said that Andy—that's my husband—was involved in an illegal activity and they won't pay for injuries or damages incurred during the commission of a crime. It wasn't really a crime. His hobby was home brewing. His stupid still blew up. It could happen to anybody. And a person is allowed to make alcohol for their own use."

"I am sure you are correct. I am not familiar with home-brewing laws."

They sat in silence for a moment. "Did you know Roberta worked for Global Insurance?" Alice smoothed her skirt several times but did not answer. "In fact, I believe that she worked in the complaint department. Did you talk to her about your problem?"

"I...didn't know that."

"Well, that is a shame. Maybe she could have helped you."

Alice made a noise that Madeline assumed was a laugh. "Help me! That woman never helped anyone but herself. Help me? I never heard anything so stupid in my life."

Madeline wondered if she was lying about not knowing Roberta worked for Global. And if it was possible that Roberta had sabotaged their claim and Alice had found out.

She was never happier to see the lights of Cross Keys coming up.

"Nice to speak with you," she said to Alice as the bus pulled up to the stop.

Alice smiled weakly. "Have a good evening."

CHAPTER 26

Billy felt like he was going in circles. The Grickly case was dead in the water for now. Tom had not been able to discover anything new in the ledger, and unless he could get more out of Bart's friends from the gym, he had no new leads. So, he decided to concentrate on Roberta's murder. At least he had witnesses and suspects for it. He had grown to believe Matt was his best suspect, but he needed evidence. He decided he needed to speak to Samantha and Fern again, since they had been Roberta's closest friends.

Samantha greeted the chief at the door with a pleasant smile. "It is so nice of you to come visit, Billy. I just took chocolate chip cookies out of the oven. I wonder if I could interest you in cookies and a cup of coffee?"

"You don't have to ask me twice."

After he was installed at the kitchen table with coffee and a plate of cookies in front of him, Samantha asked, "And so to what do I owe this visit, Billy? I hope you have found the murderer."

"I wish I could tell you so, but the investigation is still ongoing. I need to go over Roberta's final evening with you again. It is not uncommon for loved ones to not remember clearly after such a shock. I find people remember additional things after a little time has passed."

She sat down next to him at the kitchen table with a cup of coffee. "Of course, I want to help. Let me think." Samantha was silent for a few moments. "The evening before, she had gotten home on schedule, but she was in a foul mood. She had had a bad day at the office, and then somebody on the bus had irritated her, which was pretty much a daily occurrence. We ate in front of the TV because the Knicks game was on, and we both love them so much. I thought that that might improve her mood, but unfortunately they were not playing well, and they lost. It wasn't even a close contest. Naturally, Roberta went crazy, calling every player and the coach by names that a lady would not repeat. My sister was very invested in sports. But, of course you know about her betting."

Billy nodded as he ate a cookie.

"Later that night, I walked into the kitchen to see her chopping up jalapeño and habanero peppers and putting them in a plastic container. She mentioned they were for the bus party the next day. It was to be Mexican. She said that the rest of the regulars probably wouldn't bring food with enough heat for her, so she decided to bring her own."

"She did this often?"

"Oh, yes. She just loved hot peppers and added them to any food she thought was bland. She would even take them to restaurants. My sister had exacting habits regarding food."

"I see. Can you remember anything else about that night?"

Samantha paused and looked surprised. "Yes, there was a phone call from our cousin, Kate. I answered it, and she was crying. I put it on speaker so that we could both talk to her at once. She said that Matt had called her and was acting 'funny,' as she put it. He called her regularly to check on the kids, but this time he was not at all like his usual placid self. They got into an argument about the entire situation, including when and how often he was allowed to visit the boys. The call had ended with him threatening to fight her for custody of the boys if she decided to divorce him. Kate said she had never heard him that angry, and she was frightened."

"What was Roberta's reaction?"

"I'm sure you can imagine. She never liked Matt, and ever since he'd been forced to borrow some money from her, she really had no use for him. I make a point of not interfering in other people's lives."

"But not Roberta."

"Unfortunately not. She said that she would discuss it with Matt and told Kate not to worry. She said she would 'fix it.' I don't know if she had a chance to speak with him."

"But it probably would not be a friendly conversation, I would guess. What happens to the loan now that she is dead?"

Samantha sighed. "I have to decide what to do. For now, I'm just letting the payments go on as usual, and I'll make a decision after the will is settled."

* * *

Fern lived in a less prestigious private community called Heavenly Woods that bordered Whispering Pines. As Billy drove along, he couldn't help but notice that the homes were not as nice or as well maintained as those in Whispering Pines. Fern's house was a small ranch with no discernible style. The yard was small and neat but sparsely landscaped with few decorative plants. There was a forlorn, wispy maple tree standing alone and two overgrown forsythia bushes on either side of the ugly cement steps.

He saw a light on and went up to the front door. He pushed the doorbell button, but he could not hear it ring and so he knocked. There was still no answer, but he could hear what sounded like a drum beat. There was no response to his knock, so he walked around to the back door and tried the bell there. This time, he heard it ring and waited patiently, looking at the pile of old magazines and newspapers she must have been planning to recycle for the last two years. He figured there must be community rules about the front of the house being neat and free of garbage. A pale face peeked out the window, and Fern opened the door. She was holding a drum.

"Hello, Chief West."

"Hi, Fern. Sorry to bother you this late." He looked at the drum. "I can come back if you are busy."

"Oh, no! Please come on in."

Billy stepped into the kitchen. It was a mess. The sink was full of dirty dishes, and the counters were covered with old food spills. The table was piled high with junk of all kinds.

"Please excuse the mess."

"No worries."

She led him through to what he supposed was the living room, but there was no furniture, just large pillows and what at first glance looked like a least twenty heavily scented candles. The room's only decorations were pictures and figurines of unicorns.

"Aren't you afraid the house will burn down with all these candles lit at once?"

Fern laughed. "Oh! No, I don't keep them lit all the time, only when I'm doing my meditation or tarot reading or yoga exercises or drumming. Just make yourself comfortable."

Billy was puzzled as to how he might do that and finally noticed a beanbag chair and decided to try it. It was fairly comfortable, even though it made it hard for him to sit up and take notes.

"How are you feeling?"

"It's hard, but I'm getting better."

"I'm relieved. The last few times we spoke, you were very upset. I was hoping we could discuss a few things related to Roberta's death."

"I'll try."

"Since you were her best friend, I thought she might have told you things that she wouldn't tell other people."

"Oh, yes. We shared everything."

"Well, did she mention if she had had any serious arguments with anybody lately?"

"Oh, not really. People didn't understand Roberta. She only wanted to help people she knew were having problems. She was very wise, and yet people wouldn't listen. It was hard for her."

Not as hard as it was for everybody else, Billy thought.

"Anybody specifically troublesome on the days leading up to her demise?"

Fern paused, sniffled a bit as if she was about to cry but managed to control herself. "She had a running argument with her cousin's husband, Matt. Then there was Jake and Tony. They didn't get along at all."

"Did Roberta mention anything in particular about any of them?"

"No. Nothing new. I mean, she had no respect at all for Matt. She called him a pathetic excuse for a man. And she and Jake were always fighting. She just loved to tease Tony about his good looks and his marriage to a rich woman." She paused. "He can't help it if he is so handsome that women find him attractive, despite the fact that he's married." She spoke so softly that Billy had to lean toward her to hear her clearly.

"What about the women on the bus?"

"Oh, you know, just girl stuff and a few catty comments. Most of the women keep to themselves."

Billy nodded. He knew Fern was flaky and so he decided it was worth asking some questions he had asked previously to see if she was consistent in her answers. "Tell me about the party. It was Roberta's idea to have Mexican food, right?"

"Yes, Robbie loved spicy food, and she suggested doing Mexican. Everyone agreed."

"But she brought her own hot peppers."

Fern nodded. "She always did that, since food was never hot enough for her."

"Do you like spicy food?"

"Not as much as Robbie did. But I do like it."

"Then, why did you bring along extra spices?"

Fern seemed to grow pale. "I brought the salsa that we always ate, and so I knew how we normally spice it up." She looked as if she were about to cry again. "We ate it with chips when we watched TV together." She sniffled.

Billy nodded. "The ingredients you added to the salsa, did you bring them from home?"

"Yes," Fern whispered.

"What were they?"

"Oh, nothing special. Mostly garlic, some oregano, and sea salt."

"You wouldn't happen to have them or the unwashed container they were in?" Billy asked hopefully. This question had been asked and answered previously, but after seeing the state of her kitchen, he decided it was worth another shot.

"Sorry, no. I threw it out. It was cracked, and I knew I couldn't use it again."

"How was Roberta feeling that day?"

"She was fine. Full of energy. That's what makes this whole thing so..." She started to tear up. "Who would want to do this to poor Roberta?"

"I don't know, Fern. That's what I am trying to find out. Thank you for your time," Billy said, as he struggled to get up from the beanbag chair.

"Let me know if I can help in any way, Chief West. I need to know what happened."

"I appreciate that."

Billy stood by the car for a few minutes trying to straighten his back and clear his head from the candles' strong scent. Another dead end, he thought as he got into his car and pulled away.

CHAPTER 27

Tom suggested to Madeline they should speak to Agatha at the Tick-Tock Lounge, since Roberta was a regular customer there and she might have overheard something useful. He was no longer going into the city daily, and Madeline was taking a few days off work; he suggested they go there for an early drink on Tuesday and then spend some time going over what they had each found out over the past few days. They had started to discuss it over the phone but decided to wait until after they had spoken to Agatha. They met on High Street and walked the few blocks north to the Tick-Tock Lounge.

"You must be Agatha. I've heard a lot about you," Madeline said rather inadequately as she stared up at the majestically beautiful woman who looked back at her with piercing blue eyes.

"Agatha just became a grandmother," Tom said.

"Congratulations! But you don't look old enough to be a grand-mother," Madeline said.

"Thank you, dear, and your drink is definitely on the house. What can I get for you?"

"I'll have a vodka martini straight up with olives."

"Coming right up. I hear The Opossum's got a fancy, purple signature martini now." She looked at Tom with a slight smile. "Upping your game, Tom? I guess I'll have to follow suit."

"Well, certain customers were demanding something special," Tom said.

Agatha nodded and glanced at Madeline. "I see. Your usual bourbon sidecar, I assume?" Tom nodded. "So, what can I do for you folks?"

"I would like to know what you can tell us about Roberta Carlson."

"Ah, the late-lamented Roberta. You two were on the bus when she died, right? Now you are trying to figure out who killed her." Agatha placed a basket of fish-shaped crackers in front of them and smiled at Tom. "Too tempting a mystery to stay on the sidelines, huh? I am not surprised. I won't say anything to Billy."

"Gee, Tom never gives me fish crackers," Madeline observed.

"The Opossum's not as classy as the Tick-Tock Lounge. Despite its fancy cocktails."

"Is that why Roberta hung out here?" Tom sipped his drink and nodded his approval.

Agatha grimaced. "That woman drove me crazy, and she practically lived here. I don't think in all my years I have ever met anyone so devoid of even one decent human quality. God knows I tried to get her to go to some other tavern. I even physically threw her out at least a dozen times."

"I would have liked to see that," Madeline said.

Agatha laughed. "Yes, it gave me great pleasure. But she always came back. Sort of like, well—" she waved her hand along the bar "—a boomerang."

"Had Roberta been acting different in any way? Or had she been talking about anything or anybody that suggested a new focus? Or any intensifying of an old one?" Tom asked.

Agatha looked thoughtful. "I tried not to listen to her, but it was hard not to pay some attention because her voice cut through every other noise in the place. Let me think. The only recent new thing was about Tony Fowler." Agatha paused then continued. "She referred to him as a 'two timing jerk who needed to be punished'. I took that to mean she believed that he was cheating on his wife and that she wanted to find out with whom and confront him with it. As always, I could never figure out her angle, but it just seemed to make Roberta happy to make other people miserable and usually over something that was none of her business."

"Did she ever talk about her sister?" Tom asked.

Agatha smiled. "Oh, yes, the sister. Sickly Sweet Samantha she called her. Roberta was very strange about her sister. As I'm sure you two know, usually you knew right away what she felt about a person, but not the sister."

"What did you think she felt about Samantha?" Tom asked.

"I always thought that Roberta was afraid of her sister. But maybe that's too strong a word. She respected her sister. Probably the only person in the world she considered her equal."

"What made you think that?"

Agatha carefully wiped the bar as she spoke. "I don't know precisely, but never in my hearing did she make a truly negative comment about Samantha which, as I'm sure you know, is uncharacteristic of Roberta. Don't get me wrong, she didn't say anything good either. From what I could gather, if Samantha said *Jump!* Roberta might not have said *How high?*, but she did jump."

"So how frightened do you think she was of Samantha?" Tom asked.

Agatha looked thoughtfully at him. "If you mean do I think that Samantha would murder Roberta, I honestly don't know. I have never met Samantha. I know I would have if I was Roberta's sister and roommate. And she is from the same gene pool, so who knows, maybe she is equally nasty. In a sickly sweet sort of way."

"Did she ever bring her friend Fern with her or talk about her?" Madeline asked.

Agatha laughed. "Oh, yes, Fern was here frequently. I thought of Fern as Roberta's pet. Some people have dogs, cats or gerbils. Roberta had Fern."

"That's an interesting way of looking at it," Madeline said.

"I got the impression that Fern didn't mind being bossed around by Roberta. I'm not sure that she is the smartest girl in town. They argued occasionally about Fern's attraction to the wrong kind of men. Roberta would lecture her about the pitfalls of men in general and married men in particular."

"Did Fern mention she had a lover?" Madeline asked.

"Not that I heard. But Roberta would nag her anyway."

They left the Tickity and walked through town in the direction of the diner. It was a nice evening, so Tom suggested they sit on one of the benches on the library lawn. They sat side by side on a small one, overlooking a bed of heaths and heathers. Madeline leaned back, while Tom sat on the edge of the seat.

"So, you spend your night off at a bar? I would think that you'd want to go to the launderette or something else exciting," Madeline observed.

"Trust me. The Cross Keys launderette is not as fascinating as you might think."

Madeline found that she loved the investigation. Her initial trepidation had vanished. She enjoyed the time she was spending with Tom and going over the clues and suspects with him. It was thrilling to try and figure out what had really happened. She realized her excitement was a completely inappropriate response to a murder, but that's how she felt.

"I feel like we are sitting on the bus," Madeline quipped.

Tom laughed. "Yes. I think this is the smallest bench on the lawn."

"Well, Agatha was interesting," Madeline commented.

Tom nodded. "She's got her finger on the pulse of this town. The Tickity is a magnet for the rowdier locals. So do you have any new information or observations?"

"Yes, as a matter of fact I do."

Tom gave her a questioning look. "Do tell."

"I overheard an interesting conversation between Fern and Sara Beth. You know, the woman who owns the Feast of the Spirit," Madeline said.

"Why in the world would you go there?"

She shrugged and studied the plants intensely. "Oh, I was just curious. Hadn't heard much about it, so I just dropped in to see what kind of products she sells. Anyway, Fern was in there. She seems pretty close to the owner. But here's the good part. They talked about Fern's affair with a local married man. At least I assumed he was married based on what Fern said. Things like they couldn't be together when she needed him."

Tom looked interested as he leaned back on the bench next to her. "So that's why you asked Agatha if Fern mentioned a lover! No name was revealed, I assume."

"You assume correctly. But Tony did cross my mind."

"Any particular reason?"

Madeline sighed. "Not really. It's just that he is local and always seems to give Fern a lot of attention. I thought it was to annoy Roberta, but maybe that was not the only reason. And he is one of our suspects."

Tom nodded. "If it's true, Tony is pretty reckless to fool around with Roberta's best friend. He has a lot to lose if it comes out."

"I agree. Fern probably told Roberta everything."

"Maybe not. Knowing that she wouldn't approve and would cause Tony trouble, she might have kept it secret."

"Roberta alluded to him being unfaithful on the bus and now Agatha mentioned her making a direct statement and a threat to expose him. I thought it was just because he flirted with all the women. Maybe it's not Fern, or maybe she's not the only woman, and Roberta really knew something and was blackmailing him."

They sat in silence.

"I think we need the blackboard," Madeline finally said.

Tom nodded as they stood up and walked to The Opossum.

CHAPTER 28

"I think we need to take each of our suspects one by one," Madeline said as they sat down on the love seat.

"Agreed. I think we know enough now to eliminate some of them."

"I managed to speak to Alice on the bus."

"Lucky you!"

"Yes, she is a real peach. Alice's insurance problem seems pretty bad, though. Her husband's still blew up, and the insurance company won't pay because it was an illegal activity. Roberta worked for the insurance company that held the policy. Alice said she never discussed it with her."

"Yes. I found that out on the PI website. I remember when the still blew up and set the house on fire. It was the gossip of Cross Keys for at least a week. The volunteer fire department had trouble putting it out. He broke every rule, including distilling indoors and not controlling the alcohol vapor. He probably made his own equipment and did a bad job of it. My guess is that he was way over the legal limit on quantity and was probably selling it. Which is also illegal."

"How do you know so much about home brewing?"

"I do own a bar."

"Ah. True. I think it seems odd Alice would allow him to make the devil alcohol, and in her own home no less. Since she 'can't abide alcohol,' as she puts it."

"Maybe she liked the idea of making money more than she hates alcohol. Alice is strange and possibly dangerous, but she is not stupid. She must have known that Roberta wouldn't help her with the claim. If what she says about not telling Roberta about the claim is true, Alice really had no reason to be angry with her, other than having to sit next to her on a daily basis and listen to her snide comments."

Tom moved to the blackboard and crossed her name off the list of suspects.

"I think that Matt is innocent also. I ran into him at Bolter's. He bought a handful of lottery tickets. He seemed pretty depressed, mostly about his family problems."

"If he is trying to get back with his family, he might have been desperate enough to do it," Madeline said.

Tom tapped the blackboard with his chalk. "Even if he believed his debt would be wiped out with Roberta's death, I still don't think he has it in him to commit a crime like this."

"Poor Matt. He sounds like a mess."

"Yes, he is a mess. But on the surface, he's got the best motive. That makes him Billy's prime suspect."

"Did you speak with Billy about it?"

"Yes. I told him about Matt walking off with Roberta's green tote the night of the party. He found that very interesting."

"What about Jake?"

"I think we can rule out Jake too. Roberta caused him a lot of trouble in his business and personal life but not enough to kill her. He's a practical guy. Seems to me to be a really nice guy too. He's just glad she's gone."

"I agree, based on what we know. He seemed to just let her nasty comments wash over him."

"So, we can eliminate Matt and Jake?" Madeline nodded. Tom crossed them off.

"What about Samantha? Are we keeping her on our short list?" Madeline asked.

Tom looked thoughtful. "My gut says no. They may have had their differences, but no information has appeared that has me believing she would be motivated to murder her only sister."

Madeline nodded. "I agree. From what you've heard from Billy, she is intent on finding the killer. That could be a cover, but let's not forget she specifically pointed out Roberta never took any drugs. Not a good setup for hiding a murder, especially since she could have made us believe that Roberta was an addict and overdosed on her own."

Tom smiled at her. "Excellent point. Let's strike her off."

"What about Fern?" Madeline asked.

"Not sure. It seems unlikely she'd be involved. Unless..."

"Unless what?"

"Someone used her. Spiked her spices without her knowing it. It's a long shot, though."

Tom sat down on the love seat and leaned back, brushing up against Madeline. She leaned into him slightly. "So that leaves Tony."

"I am thinking Tony is our man," Tom said softly.

"Yes, I am getting the same feeling. He has a lot to lose if it comes out he is an unfaithful husband."

"Yes, if that is what the secret is, or his only secret. I think Tony has many secrets. We need to know what Roberta had on him." They sat in silence for a few minutes, both staring at the blackboard.

"I think Fern has all the answers," Tom finally said. "We need to talk to her and get her to open up. If she put the poison in the salsa, it was not on purpose. She was tricked. She is probably terrified. I think you should call her and see if you can go to her home and talk to her. She will be more comfortable in her natural habitat."

"What is my excuse?"

"Maybe tell her you want a tarot reading about your divorce. That should make her sympathetic toward you. Since she has loved and lost a lot. Ask her if Sara Beth is a good reader or psychic. She will probably take it as a compliment you are asking her for advice. It may be the first time anybody has."

Tom's phone buzzed, and he moved to answer it. "Okay, send him up," he said and hung up. "That was Adam. Billy's downstairs and wants to talk."

"Do you want me to leave?"

"No. I think he knows what we're doing, and since you have helped me get this far you should stay," he said as he stood up and flipped the blackboard to the other side which had the bus seating chart on it. Billy nodded and smiled as he walked into the office. "Evening." He looked at the board. "I can see you two have been busy."

"Just trying to help," Tom said. "I asked Madeline to help me because she is also a witness and knows the suspects. And she is not a suspect herself."

Billy nodded. "In that case, I think it is a good time to compare notes."

"Okay. Unfortunately, we're still pursuing some leads and don't have anything concrete to offer."

"We have serious speculation," Madeline added. "But that doesn't really help you, does it?"

"No. Without any hard evidence, it comes down to who has the strongest motivation and greatest opportunity. My money's on Matt at this point."

Madeline gave Tom a knowing look. "I suppose you have a point. But why now?" Tom asked.

"That's easy. He has spent months in turmoil. He had had enough. He was being mercilessly squeezed by the loan with outrageous interest. He lives in a dumpy, one-room apartment instead of his beautiful lakeside home. A guy can only take so much, you know. Roberta was ruining his life, and he snapped."

"I don't know. Matt is a nice guy. No matter how desperate his situation, I don't think he has the temperament or the type of mind to be a premeditated murderer. Besides, he didn't know if Roberta's death would change his situation. It might be satisfying to kill Roberta but not necessarily beneficial to his situation," Tom added.

"In your opinion."

"In my opinion." Tom looked stern.

"I agree," Madeline added. "It had to be someone else. Someone who had more to lose than Matt. He had already lost what he held dear. There was no guarantee that killing Roberta would return his family to him," Madeline said.

Billy shook his head. "The poor sucker's life fell apart, and Roberta danced on its grave. Murder is not a rational thing, in most cases. Sometimes it is pure hate and blind obsession. Matt needed to blame somebody for his unhappiness, and who was more appropriate than Roberta?"

"You may have a point there," Tom conceded.

"The night before the murder, Kate called Roberta, crying, afraid and unsure of what to do. He had threatened to sue for full custody of the kids if Kate filed for divorce. It sounds to me like a guy who had snapped."

"That's just plain sad, but hardly murderous. Divorce does horrible things to people," Madeline said.

"So how did Matt put the poison in Roberta's food the night of the party?" Tom asked.

Billy looked sheepish. "Well, I think he must have put it into the container of peppers in her bag when he disappeared with it. And, by the way, thanks again for that piece of information."

"How did he know the peppers were going to be in the bag?"

"He got lucky on that one. It made poisoning her easier."

"Are you hoping that Matt crumbles into a sad heap and confesses all to you under the harsh lights of the Cross Keys police interview room?"

Billy laughed. "Well, we aren't allowed to torture suspects anymore, so it's not as effective as it used to be. But, yeah, I think he will confess if pressed."

"I agree with Tom," Madeline added. "I don't think Matt is the killer. Have you seriously considered other suspects?"

"With all due respect, you are not a seasoned criminal investigator. Your theories are fine, but I have to deal with facts. Yes, I have considered all the bus people. Matt has the best motive and the best opportunity. It is that simple," Billy said calmly but firmly.

"Maddie and I are working on another angle. Give us a little more time to see if it pans out. Matt isn't going anywhere."

Billy looked thoughtful. "Okay," he finally said. "only because I know you're good at this kind of thing. I trust you. I'll give you a few more days. The mayor is really on my butt to solve it, but I don't want to arrest the wrong person."

"Thanks. We'll do our best. I'll be in touch."

CHAPTER 29

After Billy left, they sat in silence for a moment.

"So, what is our next move?" Madeline asked.

"We have to find the real killer, and we need to do it rapidly."

"There is something I have noticed which I didn't think much about until we started discussing Fern and Tony. You haven't been on the bus regularly since Roberta's death, so you don't know about it."

"What?"

"Every Thursday evening since the remembrance luncheon, Fern gets off the bus in Port Potter. But she gets on in Cross Keys the following morning in a new outfit. Moira asked her about it, and she says she is taking a boot-camp exercise class at The Gym. A friend— she made air quotes with her fingers as she spoke the word —from the gym drives her back to Cross Keys."

"Sounds perfectly logical."

"But here's the interesting thing. Tony has been getting on and off in Lyon on Thursdays. He said his mother and sister are having problems, and he needs to spend more time with them. Moira says they live in a trailer park in Lyon."

"We need to tail both of them," Tom said immediately.

"I'll break out my trench coat and fake beard."

Tom laughed. "I think a Van Dyke would suit you. You take Fern, and I will follow Tony. We may find out something useful."

* * *

The next Thursday Madeline left in plenty of time to get to the Port Potter stop so she could find a good place to park with a view of the bus stop. Since her car was distinctive, she drove Tom's Jeep, and he borrowed Adam's truck. There was a small parking lot across the street and down a few yards from the stop that would allow her to easily follow in any direction that might be necessary.

The bus pulled in right on time, and Fern got off. She stood on the corner looking anxious and occasionally glanced toward the Lyon Bridge. Fern's whole demeanor changed to a gleeful smile as she watched a silver Mercedes AMG roadster approach her corner. Tony was at the wheel.

Madeline followed as he drove around the block and headed back to Lyon. She noticed a gray Ford pickup was following her.

Tony turned into the Lyon Liaison Motel and drove directly to the back where cars were not visible from the street. The motel was located across from a fireworks store, a smoke shop and a string of bars. The long one-story building was sandwiched between the three-lane highway and the Delaware River.

Madeline drove past the motel and into the large empty parking lot of the fireworks superstore. She did a search on her phone. According to the motel's website, it rented rooms by the hour and offered features such as hot tubs, waterbeds, mirrored walls and ceilings, and other *romantic aids for lovers.*

Tom pulled up, and Madeline joined him in the Ford's cab.

"So, we were right!" Madeline said.

"It appears so. This opens up a lot of questions."

"What do we do now?"

"No point in waiting around. We found out what we needed to know. Meet me at the bar and I will buy you a Opossumtini and we can discuss this new information."

"How can I refuse such a gracious invitation?"

Thirty minutes later, Madeline walked into The Opossum. Tom smiled and had a drink in front of her in no time. "I think we need privacy."

As she entered the office with her drink, she was surprised to see a coffee table had been placed in front of the love seat with a bowl of fish crackers sitting on it.

"You and Agatha really do compete, don't you? I saw a sign in the Tickity window advertising a special Tick-Tock Tequila Manhattan cocktail."

"I am not surprised. Agatha is very competitive." He smiled as he sat down next to her with a bourbon and ginger ale.

"This is the first time I have seen you drink in the bar."

"It is my place of business, so generally I do not drink while working."

"Well, technically you are not working."

"Technically," he smiled and took a long swallow. "Tony and Fern are lovers, and my guess is they have been for some time."

"We also know that Roberta would have hated the idea. So, are we concluding that Tony killed Roberta?"

Tom sat silently staring at the blackboard where Tony was the only name not crossed out. "I think so. If Roberta knew about their affair and threatened to expose him, it would be a powerful motive. The question is did Fern assist Tony in the murder, or did he do it on his own?"

"I continue to believe she did not help him knowingly."

"But she may be so in love, he talked her into it, and now she regrets it. You must know love can change people, even make them behave in uncharacteristic ways," he said, looking into her eyes.

"Yes, I-I know," she stammered and looked away. "What is our next move? Should we tell Billy?"

Tom was silent for a few seconds. "Not yet. We need more information. I think if you approach Fern in the right way, you can get information out of her."

"Okay. As you suggested, I will call her up and tell her I am having trouble with my divorce and I want to know more about Sara Beth's fortune-telling abilities."

"No. Now that we know more about her affair, tell her you want advice from Sara Beth about your love life."

"Really? I have a love life?"

Tom smiled at her. "That will titillate her, and she will want to know more and be anxious to talk to you. When she presses you, tell her you and I are getting serious, and you need to know if it is the real thing or just a fling to me. After all, you were badly hurt by your husband's betrayal. Right up her alley."

"Should I just make up details about our relationship? She might gossip about it to other people."

Tom laughed. "That won't be the first time that has happened to me. Don't worry, there is already gossip about us."

"What?" Madeline was mortified.

"Of course. We have been inseparable for days. And you come into the bar, and we disappear up here. People don't know we have a blackboard and not a bed. Think of Harry and Jeff. I thought they were going to ask me if my intentions were honorable."

Madeline felt her face grow warm. She wondered if he had been reading her mind about her desire for their friendship to be more. "So, are you a gentle and sweet lover, or a bit rough and dom-ineering?" she asked, hoping she sounded less shaky than she felt.

"Whatever you would prefer, my dear."

CHAPTER 30

Billy walked into the Tickity on Saturday morning with low expectations. Agatha greeted him and led him over to a corner table.

"Billy, this is Odell Owens. Odell, this is Chief West. Odell is my assistant cook and chief bottle washer, and he does the basic cleaning also. Right, Odell?"

Odell shrugged his shoulders and looked bored. He was young, with uncombed stringy dark hair and an unhealthy-looking pasty-white complexion. There was a barbell piercing through his eyebrow, and he had several rings in one ear; his arms were covered with vividly colored tattoos. He wore black jeans and a thin, frayed dingy white T-shirt with a band logo on it. He was sitting hunched over, staring down, with his forearms on the table, his ringed fingers clasped in front of him.

"Hello, Odell," Billy said as he sat down. Agatha put a glass of Coke in front of him then joined them. Billy nodded his thanks.

"Agatha tells me you have some information that might be helpful about the night Bart Grickly was murdered."

Odell shrugged again. "Maybe," he mumbled.

"It is sometimes hard to get him to say much," Agatha said. "Odell, please just tell Chief West what you told me. Simple as that. You are not going to get in any trouble. Right, Billy?"

"That's right. I am just interested in what you have to say," Billy said and smiled. "I will keep it totally confidential." He sat back in the chair and put his notebook and pencil down on the table in front of him.

Odell shook his head and ran his fingers through his hair. His hand fell back down onto the table, his heavy rings landing with a thud. He fingered the spiritual bead bracelet on his left wrist. He slowly looked up at Billy without raising his head. "I was bringing up a bag of onions from the basement for the cook. The door from the basement is at the end of the small hallway near the restrooms. As I passed the men's room, I heard two men arguing. I stopped to listen, to see if it was going to escalate, because Agatha doesn't like fighting in her bar."

Billy nodded.

"I recognized Bart Grickly's voice. He's here all the time. Bart was yelling at some guy. I couldn't hear the other guy's voice too clear."

"Then what?"

"There was a loud thump, like something hitting the wall hard, and then a moan. Bart kept yelling. The other man started to yell.

He was begging Bart to give him another chance. He said something about making good on the lost product. Bart laughed, said he would make sure he paid for it and then told him to meet him later in the alley, after closing, to work it out."

"Did you see the other man?"

"Bart opened the door and walked out. A few minutes later, the other man staggered out. It was Tony Fowler. He's a regular too."

Billy was stunned. He sat back in his chair and looked over at Agatha. "Well, I'll be damned," he finally said. "Why did you wait so long to come forward?"

Odell sat up and leaned back in his chair. "I didn't know about Bart. I left town early the next morning. Took a road trip with my girlfriend. I just got back and found out what happened. I mentioned what I seen to Agatha, and here we are."

Billy nodded. He had been trying to contact the young man as part of the interview process; he had been on the list as a follow-up interview. But he could see having Agatha with him helped Odell talk. "Did you see or hear anybody else arguing with Bart?"

There was a long silence, but Billy waited patiently.

"No. I am mostly back in the kitchen. Is that all, Chief?"

"Yes. If you think of anything else, let me know." He gave him his card. "And thank you for coming forward. It's important."

Odell stood up and headed back to the kitchen.

Billy looked at Agatha with a broad smile. "Aggie, I could kiss you!"

Agatha laughed. "But you know better than to try, right?"

"Thanks, Agatha. Don't tell anybody about this please."

"Of course. Glad I can help."

Billy sat in his patrol car thinking for a long time and then headed over to The Opossum. Tom was working until Adam came in later, so their conversation was frequently interrupted, which frustrated them both.

"Tony Fowler and Bart Grickly? That could explain a lot," Tom said.

"What do you mean?"

"So, the rumors that he was on a strict allowance and needed extra income must have been true. I know Tony liked to gamble. He talked about it when we worked out together at The Gym, so my guess is Tony was gambling with Bart and must have got in over his head and maybe started selling drugs to cover it. That may have been the product referenced in the argument."

Billy nodded. "Yeah, Bart would front him the product, and then Tony would pay him when he sold it. I heard from another source that Bart liked to make this kind of selling arrangement. And he was merciless if the seller didn't fulfill their part of the bargain. Broken hands and bashed knees could result."

"Man, he had to be careful! If his wife and the judge found out he was dealing drugs, he'd lose everything."

"Yeah, I got that far myself." Billy said.

"Bart could have threatened to tell Olivia or to physically harm him."

"Tony decided he had to kill Bart. Solves all the problems, gets rid of his debt and stops Bart from exposing him. Odell's statement puts him there at the right time."

"Yeah. Sounds reasonable."

"I have Odell's statement, but it would be good if I could really connect Tony to Bart with solid evidence, like finding him in Bart's betting book."

"Bart and Tony both grew up in Lyon, didn't they?" Tom asked. "Did they grow up in the same trailer park by any chance? Do they go back that far?"

"I don't know," Billy mumbled.

"They played football in high school together. There's a team photo in Bart's book."

Billy gave Tom a puzzled look.

"Maybe Tony is one of the names in the ledger. I've got the copies in my office." Tom signaled Adam, who had just arrived, to watch the bar and led Billy up to his office. He took the papers from the envelope and spread them out on the coffee table. "Let's see if any of the nicknames ring a bell."

They went through the betting list, but nothing seemed to stand out. Then they focused in on the Specials.

"*Romeo!*" they said in unison.

"How the hell did we miss that? Look at the dates. They must be when he gave Tony the drugs, and they lead right up to a week before the murder. And the letters must be the drugs. *Z* would be for Xanax. Zanbars or Zannies they call it sometimes. *O* would be the oxy. Wow. We cracked the code," Billy said excitedly.

"Do you think Roberta knew about Tony's debts and was squeezing him as well?"

"Possible." Billy sighed deeply and sat back on the love seat. "According to Joelle, she barged in while Bart was with another client. And she knew the client. It could have been Tony."

"So, maybe the two murders are connected?"

"Sounds like I need to have another talk with Tony."

"Sounds like. Meanwhile, Maddie and I are working another angle. Could break open the whole thing?"

"Want to share?"

"Not yet, but soon. I'll keep you posted." After Billy left, Tom called Madeline and told her about the new information from Odell.

"If Tony murdered Grickly, and maybe Roberta, Fern could be in some serious danger," Madeline said. "We have to warn her!"

"If we do, she'll probably tell Tony and be in more danger. He's a desperate man."

"So, we do nothing?"

"At this point, we need to leave it to Billy. He's probably got enough to detain Tony."

"And what if he doesn't?"

"Then, we go to him with our information and get her protection."

"Okay…I guess. Let me know what happens." She hung up.

But Madeline wasn't convinced. Fern was vulnerable. She knew what she had to do.

CHAPTER 31

Fern sat in her living room in total silence. No mood music, no drumming and no candles. She was writing in her unicorn journal. So much was going on in her head that she needed to make some sense out of it by writing it all down. She discovered she needed more light and she could not write comfortably sitting on the beanbag or piles of pillows, so she brought in a floor lamp and a chair from the kitchen and put a pillow on her lap to raise the journal to a comfortable height for writing.

At first, she attempted to write with the quill pen and bottled ink that Sara Beth had sold her. The feather was a deep green, and it had come with a stand, extra nibs, and ink in a dark brown craft box with a satin tie. She could not get it to work properly: smudges and puddles of ink were all over the clean white pages of her journal. So, she switched to a ballpoint pen.

Fern had been surprised when Madeline called her, but she was very curious to know what the personal subject was that she wanted to discuss. She was sure it had something to do with Tom. She figured she would have to be brutally honest with Madeline about her chances with him. She felt bad about having to dash her hopes and even made a note about it in her journal.

Madeline had some trouble finding the house. The community was a never-ending maze of streets with similar-looking houses, and all the street names seemed to start with S. She drove around, becoming more and more lost, until a dry-cleaning delivery van driver told her precisely how to find Fern's house. She rang the bell, but hearing nothing, she knocked.

"Hi, Madeline. It's nice to see you," Fern greeted her as she opened the door. "Please come in. I hope you didn't have trouble finding the house. Some people get confused."

"No. Your directions were perfect. Thanks for making the time for me, Fern. I really appreciate it."

Fern showed her into the living room. Madeline looked around. The decor of pillows, a beanbag, candles, unicorn prints, a plain wooden chair, and a floor lamp seemed perfectly suited to Fern.

"Your place is so cozy and comfortable," Madeline gushed.

Fern nodded and smiled at the compliment.

"Can I get you herbal tea?"

"That would be lovely," she responded. Madeline followed her to the kitchen, which was a mess with half-empty fast-food containers scattered on the counter and dirty dishes filling the sink. But the mugs for the tea came out of the dishwasher and were still warm.

"I never get around to cleaning up." Fern waved her hand around in the air encompassing the kitchen. "There is no time with the commute and other things." She handed Madeline her tea. "I guess I'm just a slob."

"Oh, no. I have the same problem."

"You do?"

Madeline nodded. "Cleaning and neatening things up are the last things I ever manage to do."

They sat on pillows facing each other in the living room and sipped their tea in silence for a few moments.

"So," Fern said, "to what do I owe this visit?"

"Well, I am going through a divorce, as you know."

"Yes. Been there done that—twice," Fern added.

"Well, I am not really mourning my marriage so much as trying to figure out how to move on to a new relationship."

"It's tough. Believe me, I know. If it weren't for Roberta and Sara Beth, I'd be a mess."

Madeline couldn't help thinking *Really?* but didn't show it and just nodded.

"That's sort of why I'm here. I heard you talking to Sara Beth the other day in the store and how much she helped you. I was thinking maybe she could help me."

"It's Tom, isn't it?"

"Uh. We have a lot in common," Madeline said vaguely.

"So the fact he is handsome and sexy has nothing to do with it?" Fern giggled.

"So...here's the thing. It's starting to get serious, at least for me, and I just want to be sure it is going to work out before, you know, I get carried away. I'm nervous because of my divorce. I thought I knew my husband, but I didn't, really. I don't trust myself. Maybe I am misunderstanding what Tom is feeling."

"Oh, you should be careful. Robbie always said he is a love 'em and leave 'em kind of guy. He could break your heart, and that is not what you need now. Trust me, I know. But Sara Beth can definitely help you." She gave a big sigh and took a deep, cleansing breath. "She is a great spiritual guide. She has been advising me on meditation. She said a calm mind would make me more receptive to true love. She also did tarot-card readings that were so on-target it is unbelievable. You should definitely consult her. I am sure she will help you as much as she has helped me. I needed her support because Roberta never supported my quest for love."

"Oh, really? I am surprised. You both seemed so close. I just assumed she wanted to see you happy."

"We were, but, well, she didn't much care for my choice in men. Like my current love. She would have hated him, mostly because he's married."

"Yes. That does make a relationship tricky."

"She didn't understand how much we love each other." Fern had a joyous expression on her face. "He swept me off my feet like a real Prince Charming. He was so romantic. He pursued me and gave me gifts and told me how beautiful I am. I mean, we fell deeply in love."

"So, Roberta didn't know?"

Fern shook her head. "No. I think she might have suspected, but I had to keep it secret. For him."

"But it must be frustrating that you can't be together whenever you want. Especially right now."

"Yes! Oh, you do understand. We are star-crossed lovers. Our love has to be a secret from everybody. It's precious moments, really. His wife can't find out until his affairs are in order and he can move out." Fern paused as she looked down and picked at her nail polish. "We're going to run away together, start a new life. It is so hard to see each other every day but to have to be distant. We are so close together yet so far apart." Fern put her hand over her mouth. "Oh, I shouldn't have said that."

Madeline decided to go for it. "Tony?"

Fern looked astonished but finally nodded.

"I don't blame you. He is extremely handsome, and he obviously is very into you. But I have a feeling there is more to this story."

Fern stared at her. "You are very insightful. Yes, there is more." Relieved to finally unburden herself, everything came out in a rush of words. "Unfortunately, he is a gambler and got into some trouble with that awful Bart Grickly. I warned him to be careful. I knew Roberta had had some run-ins with him, but she was strong enough to handle him. No one screwed around with her. But Tony isn't like her. He's sensitive, and he had a lot to lose. Grickly threatened to expose his gambling debts to his wife unless he started to do things for him. You know, illegal things."

"That doesn't sound good. What kind of things?"

"Oh, he never really told me. He said it was safer for me not to know. He is so protective." She gave a soft sigh. "It has been really hard for him. And it got worse after Grickly was found dead. He was so stressed about it. I thought he'd be relieved, but it was the opposite. Yet, despite it all, he is so thoughtful. Like for the Spring Soiree, I forgot to bring the garlic salt and spice blend for the salsa, and I couldn't get away from work to get the ingredients, so he made it for me and said he added something special that made it even better for Roberta."

"I remember Roberta liking it so much that she ate the rest of it before anyone could have any."

Fern nodded and sniffed. "She loved it, just as he said she would. Now she's gone."

"He must have comforted you in your grief over Roberta. I bet that helped you."

Fern looked thoughtful. "It's strange. He seemed almost relieved about her passing. I guess it was because he was worried that she'd find out and tell me to break up with him."

"Probably. How are things with him now?"

"We spend private time together every week, but he's not talking so much about the future. He says he's got a lot on his mind."

I'll bet, Madeline thought.

"Fern, you know, it might be smart to share the information about the spices with the police."

"I did already. Except—"

"Uh, Fern, I don't want to be negative, but did you ever think that what Tony gave you might have contributed to Roberta's death?" Madeline knew she was on shaky ground.

"Do you really think it had anything to do with Robbie's death?" Fern sounded panicked.

"I don't know, of course, but it may have."

All the color drained from Fern's already pale face. "Oh. I don't understand. Could I be in trouble? I told Billy that I made the spice blend so nobody would guess we are a couple. Tony did it just for me."

"Oh, Fern! You need to tell the police the truth."

"Oh, no! I don't know what to do." Her eyes filled with tears.

She sniffled and composed herself. "Maybe I'll ask Tony what's best to do," she said brightly as if this solved the problem.

"No. No, I don't think that is such a good idea. Fern, I am truly sorry, but you need to face the fact that Tony may have put the drugs in the spices."

Fern's expression went from worried to terrified. "Oh, no! Why would he do that? No, no. He's not a murderer. He wouldn't do that to me. He loves me more than anything in the world. And that would mean I killed my best friend in the world." She was wringing her hands, and tears began to drip down her checks.

"Maybe he had problems you didn't know about."

"But he did insist I bring the salsa. He knew me and Robbie ate it all the time, and I told him about how we added things to make it superhot." Fern looked beseechingly at Madeline.

"Well, if you come forward with this information, I can go with you to see Chief West, if you want. You know, for moral support. Or maybe you need a lawyer."

"Really? You would do that? That would make me feel more comfortable. That's really nice of you. I don't know any lawyers."

They sat in silence, and both of them jumped when Fern's cell phone rang with a happy, chiming sound.

"Oh, no! It's him! What should I do? I said I would be home, and he said maybe we could get together."

Madeline was flustered. She was unsure how to handle the situation.

By the time Fern found the phone, the call had gone to voice mail, and Fern played it. "Oh, he is waiting for me at our usual place. I always meet him when he calls me. Always!" Fern sounded panic-stricken.

"Where is that?"

"The Liaison Motel, in Lyon, room three."

"Okay. Calm down. It will be fine. You should meet him as planned. Text him back to say you'll be there. I'll call Billy and tell him to meet you both there so you can clear it all up together."

"Let me talk to him first."

"But—"

"Madeline, trust me. My eyes are open now," Fern said as she texted Tony back. "Will you follow me there, though?"

"Follow you? Me? I'm not sure—"

"I would feel better if I knew you were there. You can sit in your car. Please!"

"Okay…I guess so," Madeline said uneasily. She was feeling that the situation was getting dangerous.

"Thanks for being so understanding. You came to me for advice, and now look at us. I need to get dressed. I always wear a sexy outfit."

It took her just a few minutes to put on a short tight black sequined dress and red stilettos. A few minutes more to refresh her makeup and splash on perfume.

"What do you think?" Fern asked, spinning around like a runway model.

"Very sexy," Madeline responded, hoping she didn't sound as nervous as she felt.

As she drove to the motel, she thought she should at least call Tom and tell him what was happening. Her call went to voice mail, and she left a brief message that Fern had confirmed that Tony had put the poison in the spices that killed Roberta. She was going with Fern to the motel in Lyon to confront him in room three and asked him to send Billy immediately. She was regretting she didn't have Billy's cell number.

CHAPTER 32

Madeline followed as Fern drove around to the back of the motel and parked in a spot behind the office, which was a separate building from the long, low structure of motel rooms. Fern parked next to Tony's silver Mercedes.

She wobbled over to Madeline on her high heels. "I think I should go in alone. I'll talk to him, and then I'll text you. I think he will clear it all up, and you can leave. If not, I will tell you to call the police. Does that sound like a good plan?"

"Uh, I thought we were going to call Chief West after you spoke to Tony."

"Maybe. Let me see what he has to say."

Madeline didn't like it. Fern was obviously going on the assumption that Tony was innocent and harmless. "Okay, but don't stay in there too long without letting me know what's happening. Once he understands you know what he did, it might be dangerous."

Fern gave her a quivering smile. "Despite everything I know, he really loves me, and he would never hurt me."

"I hope you're right. Be careful."

Madeline sat in the car holding her phone and wishing Tom would call or text her. Or, better yet, show up with Billy. She was getting antsy when Fern texted her to come in. She was scared but couldn't think of anything else to do. Just to be safe, she texted Tom one word, *Help*, as she got out of the car and walked slowly to the room.

She knocked on the door. It opened immediately. Tony stood in the doorway glaring at her and then grabbed her arm and pulled her inside. He kept hold of her arm, twisting it behind her as he pulled her toward him, so her back was against him. Fern was lying on the bed facedown, crying hysterically. When she looked up, Madeline could see her nose was bleeding, and one eye looked swollen.

Madeline wasn't sure, but Tony seemed high. She had noticed his pupils were dilated, and he seemed nervously excited.

"You just couldn't leave it alone. You and Tom. I knew you were snooping around. It was none of your business," he hissed into her ear. The musky sweet scent of his cologne was overpowering.

"Tony, be reasonable. You don't want to make it worse." She hoped she sounded more confident than he felt.

"Worse!" he yelled. "Things couldn't possibly get worse. Thanks to you."

"The police are on the way. I called them from the car."

"The police! That idiot Chief Billy West. He'll get here too late for you two." He pulled out a knife, flipped it open and pressed it against Madeline's neck.

"Let her go, Tony," Fern yelled. "She was just trying to help me. Please!"

"Shut up, you stupid bitch!"

Tony laughed so hard at Fern's astonished expression that Madeline thought she might be able to escape, but as she tried to twist away, he tightened his grip, and she felt the knife cut into her neck. His grasp on her was firm. She was surprised at how strong he was. Pain was radiating from her shoulder to her wrist. She was totally helpless. She felt blood running down her neck.

"You ruined everything," he said, tightening his grip. "Fern would be floating down the Delaware by now, and I would be off the hook. Now—"

The sound of cars coming to a skidding halt on the gravel parking lot outside the room startled Tony. He pulled Madeline over to the window, knife at her throat, and looked out. "Shit," he said under his breath when he saw the police cars. He threw her down to the floor, knocking her head against the wooden TV console. He ran out the door, dodged Officer Smithfield's attempt to tackle him and headed toward the river.

Madeline tried to get up but found she was dizzy and collapsed back onto the floor. Fern was crying hysterically with her face buried in the pillow.

Tom burst through the door.

"He ran," Madeline said weakly.

"Yeah. He won't get far. Are you both okay?" Tom asked.

Madeline nodded, holding her neck.

"An ambulance is on the way. Stay here. Both of you," Tom said as he followed Billy and Smithfield toward the river.

After a few minutes, gunshots rang out.

* * *

Bright lights lit up the parking lot as two police cars and two ambulances filled the space. Tony was soaking wet; his leg was bleeding from a gunshot wound. The paramedics strapped him onto a gurney and put him in one the ambulances. It sped off, followed by one of the police cars.

Fern and Madeline sat in the room while paramedics examined them. Both women were sniffling but trying to be strong. Madeline had a gauze bandage on her neck and an ice pack on her head. Fern had an ice pack covering her eye and nose.

"They'll be fine," one of the paramedics said to Tom and Billy. "Only superficial wounds."

Tom and Billy stood shaking their heads in disbelief. "Can you two please tell us how this happened?" Billy finally asked.

Madeline glanced at Fern, who sat hunched over, looking defeated. "Tom and I deduced that Tony was the killer, and we thought Fern knew more than she was saying," Madeline began. "I went over to Fern's to talk to her. She told me about her affair with Tony. She also told me he had given her the plastic container of spices she had added to the salsa. She had no idea they were poisoned." She adjusted her ice pack and quickly explained how she ended up at the motel and how Tony had grabbed her.

"I didn't believe he had set me up to poison Roberta," Fern added. "I wanted to talk to him about it. Give him a chance to explain. He got really angry. He called me all kinds of horrible names. He said he never loved me!" she wailed in despair. "Then he hit me! I told him about Madeline being outside, and he grabbed my phone and texted her to come in. I am so sorry."

She looked beseechingly around the group. "I didn't know how evil he was. I killed my best friend! And for what? For a no-good man who never loved me and wanted to kill me and throw me into the Delaware when he was finished using me. Like a...like a piece of trash." Fern broke down in violent sobs.

Billy put his hand on her shoulder. "It's over now. But I'll need both of you to come to the station to give a full statement. Let's go back to Cross Keys. I'll drive Fern. Tom, you can take Madeline. One of us can bring them back for their cars later," Billy said as they left the room.

Tom and Madeline drove in silence for a few minutes. Madeline was mortified. She knew she had behaved stupidly. "Thanks for coming," Madeline finally said. "I don't know what would have happened if you and Billy hadn't shown up." She sat staring at her hands, which were clasped in her lap.

"As soon as I listened to your voice mail, we left. Billy loves to save damsels in distress," Tom said and smiled at her.

"Yes. He does have that knight-in-shining-armor vibe."

"And I don't?"

"You did today, for sure." Madeline smiled at him.

"It definitely depends on the damsel. Are you sure you are all right?"

"I was worried about Fern, and I didn't want to wait anymore, so I went to Fern's to get the information we needed. It was Fern's idea about me going with her to meet Tony. I didn't think it was a good idea, but I didn't know what else to do, so I went along. It all seemed to happen so fast. I wasn't thinking clearly."

"I was wrong. Fern was in danger. You were reckless but brave."

"I'm a little shaky, and my head hurts. But I'll be fine. Poor Fern. At least the man I love didn't try to pin a murder on me and kill me."

"And he never will."

Madeline turned to look out her window as tears streamed down her face. After a few minutes, she composed herself and wiped the tears away. "Uh, what do you think will happen to Fern now?"

"I have a hunch Billy will be as lenient as he can be. If Tony confesses and she's proved an uwitting accomplice, I would guess she will get a slap on the wrist."

"Isn't she an accessory or something?"

"I don't think she was involved in the planning or execution of the murder. In fact, I don't think the drugs were in her spice container. But Billy will have to pry more information out of Tony."

CHAPTER 33

It did not take Billy long to get the full story from Tony, especially after the judge applied additional pressure.

Madeline took some vacation time to stay at home and recover her equilibrium. She was physically bruised and more upset than she had led Tom to believe. She'd never been in a life-threatening situation before, and it had shaken her to the core; she was also embarrassed at her stupidity. Adding to that, she had broken trust with Tom by not telling him what she was planning. He said he understood, but did he? He hadn't spoken to her since that day. She figured that any chance of a romantic relationship with him was now impossible, and she doubted their friendship was going to survive without the murder investigation keeping them in constant contact.

Her emotions kept shifting from hopeful happiness to doubt. She had noticed the way Tom kept looking at her with a slight smile and at times made comments that seemed flirtatious, and on those occasions, she could easily believe he had deeper feelings for her. But then she would think he probably had charmed many women with that same look and enigmatic smile and figured she was deluding herself by thinking she was special to him. Her divorce was due to be finalized soon, and she was reluctantly contemplating the need to make plans to return to Manhattan. She admitted to herself she didn't want to stay in Cross Keys with Tom so close and unattainable. It had just been a stupid schoolgirl romantic fantasy.

She perked up when Tom finally called.

"How are you feeling?"

"On the mend, I guess. How about you?"

"Now that it's over, I'm happy to get back to normal. I had a ton of work at the bar to catch up on. Are you up for a little excursion tomorrow?"

"Where?"

"Just dinner at a friend's house. You're my plus one."

Madeline paused for a moment. "Sure. Sounds great."

"Good, I'll pick you up around five."

"See you then." Madeline hung up. Maybe things with Tom were not as bad she thought.

The next day, she tried to appear normal and hoped her nervousness was not obvious when she got into his car. "You didn't tell me where we are going."

"Billy's house."

"Wow! Now, that's a surprise."

Tom smiled. "Billy's a great cook. It'll be fun."

After a twenty-minute drive up Franklin and then down an uninhabited gravel and dirt road, Tom pulled into a long steep paved driveway lined with walnut trees. At the top of the hill stood a two-story stone colonial house. A white picket fence surrounded an immaculate lawn with neatly pruned shrubs, dogwood trees, a very large white birch tree and a fishpond surrounded by local stone. Lush rhododendrons with smaller azaleas in front stood in neat flower beds next to the house. A winding brick walkway led to a dark green front door set into a small portico. Matching green shutters bordered the white mullion windows.

"Not what I expected," Madeline said.

"Billy inherited it from his grandmother. He grew up in this house."

Sitting in the middle of the lawn was a large white dog with orange ears and freckles on its nose. Around one of its droopy eyes, it had an orange patch of fur. As soon as the dog saw Tom get out of the car, he ran to him.

"Oh, how cute!" Madeline exclaimed as she beckoned the dog. "What kind of dog are you?"

Wagging his tail furiously, the dog sniffed Madeline in passing as it lumbered up to Tom and drooled on his pants. He reached down and scratched behind the floppy ears. "This is Delilah. She is a Clumber spaniel and the love of Billy's life."

Tom knocked on the door using the antique-brass dragonfly knocker. After a minute, Billy opened the door wearing jeans, sneakers, a T-shirt and an apron that read *Kiss the Cook*. In one hand he carried an orchid displaying two large pale violet blossoms.

"Tom! Madeline! Come on in." Delilah sped pass them into the house. "I see you met Delilah."

"She's beautiful," Madeline exclaimed.

They followed Billy along a central hall. As they walked, Madeline peeked into a formal living room on one side and a formal dining room on the other, both furnished with what she assumed were family heirlooms. Paintings varied from still lifes to hunting scenes to period portraits. Vibrantly colored and ornately patterned oriental rugs rested on the highly polished walnut floors. They arrived in the kitchen with its attached solarium. The solarium contained a varied collection of orchids, some with spectacular flowers, and presented a view of a large lawn sloping downhill, ending at a small lake bordered by extensive woods. The setting sun cast a beautiful orange glow on the surface of the lake. A freshly baked pie sat on top of the stove sending a delicious aroma into the room.

"You have a lovely home, Billy."

"Thank you. I grew up here. My grandmother had great taste."

"I can see that."

Billy smiled broadly. "I try to keep it up. Have a seat. Can I get you a drink?"

"Sure," Madeline said.

"I'll get them since I know what everybody drinks and where the alcohol is kept," Tom said as he left the kitchen.

Finally, they all sat down at the kitchen table. Delilah rested her head on Billy's lap. "I see why you wear an apron," Madeline smiled as she reached out to pet the dog's soft fur.

"Oh, it's not because of her. I was cooking." He moved the orchid to the center of the table and rested his hand on Delilah's head.

"So, we've got some time before dinner is ready. Are you ready for all the details of your first investigation? I'm happy to recap what happened, if you'd like."

"First and last, I assume."

"I'm not so sure about that," Billy said as he glanced at Tom.

"Yes, I'm dying to know the details."

"Billy needs to start," Tom said.

"Okay. Tony started with one simple problem. He needed more spending money. His paycheck was directly deposited, and Olivia gave him a strict allowance for his expenses in Manhattan. It wasn't enough for him to lead the playboy life he wanted. He was an old friend of Bart Grickly's. They grew up together in the same trailer park in Lyon, and they played football together in high school. One of Bart's businesses was being a bookmaker. Tony liked to gamble, and he assumed, like most gamblers, that he could beat the odds and make money. His luck ran hot and cold, and finally he had a really bad streak. Bart ostensibly lent him the money to cover the bets he couldn't pay. When Bart finally called in the markers and Tony couldn't pay, they made a deal. Tony would work for Bart selling drugs to pay down his debt. But he was undisciplined. Tended to party with his clients, and so he got further and further behind.

"Roberta was a regular bettor with Grickly. She barged into his house regularly looking to collect her winnings or place bets. One day she barged in while Tony was meeting with Grickly and put two and two together. Tony knew that Roberta would torture him about it. What he didn't expect was that she'd start blackmailing him to keep his secret."

"Yeah. It was hell for him," Tom added, "seeing her daily. Dealing with comments. Paying her blackmail. He was living on the edge."

"She was relentless on the bus with him," Madeline added.

"Roberta underestimated how badly cornered he felt and how desperate he was," Tom said. "After years of bullying people with no pushback, she thought she could get away with anything."

Billy nodded. "Yes. It all came to a head the night of Grickly's murder. Grickly roughed up Tony in the men's restroom at the Tickity then told him to meet him in the alley in back of the bar after closing. Tony knew the meeting was going to mean Bart had a nasty job for him to do to pay off the debt. The only way to get out from under was to get rid of Grickly. When Tony arrived at the meeting, he quietly checked out the situation. The town was dark and quiet, especially around the Tickity. Nobody was around. He saw Bart was standing with his back to the alley studying the sports page under the bar's backdoor light, so he simply snuck up to him from behind and put the rope around his neck."

"You make it sound easy," Madeline said.

"It took strength, and Tony is strong. I know—I worked out with him. But the element of surprise made it relatively easy," Tom said.

"But there is more," Billy added. "Roberta witnessed the murder."

"What? How?" Madeline exclaimed in surprise.

"You remember Roberta had won five hundred dollars on the Knicks game for both herself and her sister? She decided to let it ride on the next game, but Samantha wanted, or rather demanded, her share of the winnings. Roberta herself told me she went back out to get Samantha's money from Grickly the night he was killed. She went to his home and other joints in Port and Lyon. She drove by the Tickity on the way home. She saw Grickly's car in the alley, parked and went to find him. She rounded the corner of the Tickity and witnessed the murder. The next day, she confronted Tony, and he found out the bad news. She upped the payments on his blackmail. Of course, she didn't tell me that part. She said she never found Bart after searching in Port and Lyon."

Tom nodded. "She backed Tony further into the proverbial corner and sealed her fate. Tony figured that after Bart's death Roberta's hold over him would weaken and he could stop paying the blackmail. It would have been her word against his, and with Bart dead, no proof would have existed that she was right. The extortion would be ended. But instead, she now had an even more powerful secret to hold over him. So, Tony decided he had to eliminate Roberta. He came up with a plan involving Fern. He had started an affair with her several months before, and he knew she was in love with him and he could get her to do anything he asked her to do."

"Did he even like Fern?" Madeline asked.

Tom and Billy exchanged glances. "No," Billy said. "He was bored. He was looking for some fun, and getting away with it, nobody finding out, was like gambling, a game to him. He was planning to end it, but after Roberta started to blackmail him, he thought Fern might be useful to him in some way."

"Once the party was planned and the food theme was set as Mexican, he was good to go," Tom continued. "He made the spice mixture as a backup. He knew Fern could be flaky and might forget to bring hers. It was important she be seen adding something to the salsa. But I believed all along that the poison was not in her spices, since Fern ate some salsa after she added it. Fern did not kill her best friend."

"Really? That must have been a great relief to her."

"It was. I had to endure a sobbing Fern squeezing the life out of me and professing her undying gratitude and love. She did add the spices as we all saw, and the salsa was passed around until it got to Tony. Tony put a spot of salsa on his shirt, and then he made a big deal about cleaning it up. He took out a plain white handkerchief, which was bunched up in a ball in his jacket pocket. The crushed-up drugs were inside the handkerchief."

"Really? That out in the open? That simple? Obviously, it was easy for Tony to get the drugs. He had them from Bart Grickly, right?" Madeline said.

Tom nodded. "It didn't dawn on me at first. I knew that I had seen something that did not fit, but I could not put my finger on it. Finally, I realized that I had never seen Tony use a handkerchief. In fact, nobody uses handkerchiefs anymore for anything but as a decorative accessory. A plain white cotton one like Tony had on the day of the murder is something that belongs to his grandfather's day, not something for a hip stud like Tony to carry. Suddenly, he whips one out of his pocket. So, he dropped in the poison while fiddling around to clean his shirt. Nobody was watching him. Why would they? He stirred the drugs into the salsa with a chip and passed it back to Jake, and Jake passed it to Roberta. He knew there was no chance that Jake or anybody else would attempt to taste it."

"Thanks for that tip," Billy said. "Tony was shocked I knew about the handkerchief and how he added the poison. And if Roberta hadn't eaten it for some reason or hadn't died, he would try something else later. He really had nothing to lose," he added. "And it worked really well. Then there was the autopsy. He hadn't counted on that. He figured everybody would assume she was old and her time had come. So he was forced to use plan B, which was to push Fern under the bus, so to speak. Tony was going to force her to confess in a suicide note. He was going to drug her and push her off the Lyon Bridge, if holding a gun to her head didn't induce her to jump."

"Wow! Fern had a narrow escape," Madeline said.

"Yes, she did. It was lucky you were there. I think she would be dead if you hadn't been," Tom said as he smiled at her.

"And justice was done," Billy said, getting up from the table.

"Oh. Glad I was able to do something helpful," Madeline said, and a wave of relief overcame her as she realized she hadn't been a complete fool.

"Oh, Tom, I have Bart's yearbook you asked for."

"It is not really necessary now that you have Tony's confession and Odell's evidence, but I am curious to see if I was right." He took it and started going through it. Tom grinned and nodded. He turned the book around for Billy to see. There in the book was another photo of Bart and his group, Road Runner and the Coyotes. Each person was identified by their proper name and the nickname their teammates, or more specifically Bart, had given them. Next to Tony's name was written *Romeo*. "I didn't expect it to be so obvious. I thought it would be in an autograph or other handwritten note. That's why I wanted Bart's yearbook particularly," he explained.

"Romeo!" Billy roared.

"Yes. Tony is definitely *Romeo*."

"Hey, I have prepared a celebration dinner! I have beef bourguignon in the oven. I baked fresh French bread and have a green salad with a light vinaigrette, and I can pull one of Abigail's excellent wines out of the cellar. How does that sound?"

"Abigail?" Madeline asked.

"My grandmother. I always called her by her first name."

"And it looks like there is pie for dessert," Madeline pointed out. "Sounds delicious."

"It sounds great. Billy is a really good cook," Tom said.

"I think the word you are looking for is *chef*." Billy smiled.

"I tried to get him to work at The Opossum, but he said he preferred to fight crime not commit a culinary crime. He disapproves of hamburgers."

"Yes, you could use some help in your kitchen. But I don't hate hamburgers. I make a great one stuffed with caramelized onions and Gruyère cheese served on a freshly made brioche bun with homemade ketchup and truffle-oil French fries."

"I can see how the Opossum Burger is not up to your standards," Madeline said.

CHAPTER 34

Madeline could not believe how delicious Billy's dinner was. And the three of them had a lively, entertaining and wide-ranging conversation. After dessert, Billy brought out an excellent bottle of brandy, and they moved to comfortable chairs in the living room. Delilah joined them. After sniffing around, she finally put her large head on Madeline's lap.

"So, Billy, this seems like a good time for you to tell me about Abigail," Madeline said as she petted the dog and looked around the beautifully decorated room.

Billy smiled broadly. "Okay. To say I had an unconventional childhood is an understatement. My grandmother raised me. I never knew my parents. They died in a boating accident when I was two.

"Abigail was born into a well-to-do family from Cross Keys. This was their summer cottage. She was my fearless champion and my greatest teacher. She stopped at nothing to give me a wide exposure to the richness of life.

"One year we spent three months in Europe visiting museums, attending operas and taking cooking lessons in Paris and singing lessons in Italy. On other trips, we climbed small mountains and hiked through jungles. But she was practical too. She made me apply myself to my studies, and I ended up graduating at the top of my class. Ahead of Tom, I might add. She pushed, and yet she yielded so that I could grow at my own pace."

Billy paused, and Tom added, "Abigail was amazing. When we were young kids, she would set up treasure-hunt mysteries for us to solve. This house and the fifty acres that surround it became a tantalizing adventure land. Billy and I spent days tracking the clues she had planted. The times we solved the mysteries and found the treasures I still remember as some of the best moments of my life. The exhilaration of discovery and the satisfaction of following the chase to the conclusion was an amazing feeling."

"It sounds wonderful," Madeline said.

"After I graduated college, I applied to the FBI. I made it to Quantico, but I failed to pass all of the tests. I did not have what it takes to be a special agent. I was very disappointed and, feeling like a failure, came home to Abigail. So, she helped me get over my disappointment. We went to South America on our last big trip together. We cruised down the Amazon and visited Machu Picchu. By the time we returned, she had helped me realize that, even though I had failed to make the FBI, I still had learned a great deal and there was nothing to stop me from pursuing a career in law enforcement. So,

I ended up joining the Philadelphia PD. I had a good career and worked there for several years, and when the position of chief of police in Cross Keys opened up, I jumped on it. It was my chance to come home."

They sat in silence for a few moments.

Billy smiled forlornly. "Abigail developed dementia as she grew older. I got her the best help and care available until she died at ninety-three. She loved this house, and she died here peacefully. I loved her more than I can imagine loving any person."

Madeline nodded. "Abigail gave you her unconditional love. Many people never have that experience. You were fortunate."

Later, Tom and Madeline sat in his car in her driveway.

"That was a great evening. Solved a mystery, ate well and had fun with friends," Madeline said.

"Yes, it was a good time," Tom agreed. "Hopefully, we will enjoy many more like that. Except for the murders, of course."

"Of course. So, I will see you for dinner on Wednesday? It has been nice to have the two whole weeks at home."

"Yes, I am looking forward to it."

"It turns out I have something to celebrate!"

"Really?"

"What?"

"My divorce is final. I am a free woman at last."

"Great! We do need to celebrate that. I know it has bothered you that it took so long. Should I bring a cake?"

Madeline laughed. "Does the bakery make a *Happy Your Divorce Is Final* cake?"

"I think it's traditionally a rich chocolate cake iced with regret."

CHAPTER 35

Madeline had wanted to invite Tom to her house for dinner for quite some time. Since the start of the investigation, he had not been charging her for her meals or drinks at The Opossum so she thought this gave her a good reason to invite him for dinner as repayment and because she now felt they really were friends.

Tom was fascinated by her house. "This is a big house for one person," he observed during the tour.

"Yes, it is. I only use a small portion of it. It can make me feel lonely sometimes. I wish I could get a dog."

"Oh. Why not? They are great company. I am thinking about getting another one myself."

Madeline looked at him with one eyebrow raised. "Uh, because I commute to the city and am gone twelve hours a day. That's a long time for a dog to be alone."

Tom smiled. "Of course. But I could come walk him. Even take him with me to the bar during the day."

"Really? That would be very nice of you." Madeline smiled looking up at him.

Tom suddenly became interested in the crown molding. "This house has been maintained very well. Even the top floor and the basement are in good shape. I have seen some of these old houses that are in pitiful shape. I know they are expensive to maintain."

"Let me guess. You worked in construction too."

Tom laughed. "Actually, I worked for a man who restored Victorian houses to their original state. It was exacting work. Your house still has most of its original woodwork."

"Yes. Jeff was excited about it when he saw the inside. He says he will be happy to sell it for me whenever I am ready."

Tom stopped looking at the ceiling and looked at her with concern. "You aren't planning on selling and moving away, are you?"

"No. I am quite happy here for now. I have no plans to leave."

Tom seemed to relax and smiled at her. "I see you have been tinkering with the furnishings."

"Yes. As you can see, I haven't touched some of the spare bedrooms, but I had to modernize the living room and master bedroom. The furniture was awfully uncomfortable. I think the mattress was stuffed with horsehair. The old heavy furniture made the rooms seem dark and foreboding," Madeline said as she shivered slightly.

"Maybe you should turn it into a bed-and-breakfast."

"I don't think I could run a bed-and-breakfast and commute."

Tom laughed. "No, the B&B would be your business, and you could stop commuting."

Madeline sighed. "That is a big decision. I wouldn't know where to start."

"I am sure you could learn. Think about it."

After dinner, Madeline suggested they have a drink and sit in her living room. She sat on the end of a large comfortable sofa, and Tom took the chair next to it.

"You know," Madeline started, "you never finished telling me the story of your life. Something about your father thinking the PI job was perfect for you."

"Yes, I remember from our first bus trip together, right? Are you sure you really want to listen to it?"

"Absolutely. I am very curious."

"Okay. When I was a kid, for as long as I can remember, we had one family living in the house next door, the Wyatts. They had three children, Susan and fraternal twins Garry and Larry. The twins were mean. They were mean to each other, to Susan and to anybody they came in contact with. They were constantly injuring themselves with stupid dares and malicious taunts turning into fistfights. Susan, however, was my first love. I thought she was the most beautiful girl in the world.

"I had a couple of run-ins with the twins, but for the most part I managed to avoid them. One evening during the summer of my sophomore year in high school, my parents and I were having dinner in our kitchen, and Susan ran through the screen door screaming *Fire!* While my mother called the fire department and Susan's parents, who were at a country club dance, my dad and I ran out to find the Wyatt front porch engulfed in flames. Larry was just standing in the front yard staring at it with a weird, faraway look in his dull eyes. Garry was not around. The fire looked worse than it was, and the firemen had it all put out in a short time. They then went through the house to be sure that everything was safe.

"They found Garry in the attic bedroom the boys had shared. He was hanging by a rope from the highest rafter. A chair was lying on its side on the floor under the body. The chief of police questioned Larry. He volunteered that Garry had been depressed recently. His girlfriend had dumped him, and he had been removed from the varsity basketball team for next year. Without any further investigation, the chief pronounced it a suicide. He never dealt with how the fire started. My dad figured that was because Mr. Wyatt was the chief's lodge brother and the mayor's good friend. When I heard the story from my dad, I knew Larry was lying. Garry could not even get a girl to look at him, let alone date him, so he could not possibly have been dumped. And neither he nor his brother could play any organized group sports because they always caused a fight and ignored all the rules and any attempt to enforce them. I thought Larry was hiding the truth about what really happened.

"I told my dad about it. He was concerned and told the chief. At first, he fluffed it off but agreed to listen to my story. My dad hated the chief. Said he was a stupid and cruel man. He had treated his wife for numerous suspicious falls.

"I didn't really have anything to go on except my gut feeling. But I plunged in anyway even though the chief was glaring at me angrily. I said that the twins hated each other and always had. I had witnessed them try to hurt each other too many times to count. My guess was that they were engaged in their usual daring and taunting, and that Larry got Garry to climb up on the chair and put his head through the noose tied to the rafter and then pulled it up. Caught by surprise, Garry didn't have the time or the presence of mind to save himself. He probably kicked over the chair while thrashing around helplessly trying to regain his footing. Larry probably thought he was faking it. I could easily envision him laughing at Garry's struggle. Then, before he knew it, it was too late. His brother was dead. Once he realized what he had done, he set fire to the porch. I guess he thought the house would burn down and everybody would think that Garry died in the fire, with an unexplained noose around his neck.

"The chief went back to question Larry, who eventually told the story, pretty much the way I thought it had happened. The hanging was ruled an accident, not a suicide, and Larry was committed to a psychiatric facility for minors. He was killed there several years later during a fight with another patient."

"What about Susan?" Madeline asked.

"Well, the Wyatts moved after the incident. I never saw her again."

"Wow that is quite a story. It makes some sense why your dad supported your decision to be a PI."

"Maybe. I expect it was more about my finally settling down. And, yes, there were a couple of other situations I figured out. And no, I won't tell you now. I need to maintain some mystery," Tom said smiling at Madeline's inquisitive look.

"I told you my past was not nearly as interesting as people think. I know the gossip in Cross Keys has created a wild and lurid past, including a trail of broken hearts and even a crime of passion resulting in either the death of the other man or severe brain damage, depending on which version you hear. I think there is also a wealthy widow I supposedly married, or else I romanced her and stole all of her money. Roberta always referred to me as a drunk, when in fact I rarely drink." He looked directly into Madeline's eyes. "None of it is true. I was married once, and I have had two long-term relationships. All were my age, and none left me a fortune."

Madeline nodded slightly. "I believe you. If you never say much about yourself to other people it creates the need for people to make up stories. Of course, people will do that anyway, I guess. I have to confess to you that I really enjoyed investigating Roberta's death. You know, I didn't think I would, but I did. You're a good partner. Easy to be with."

Tom smiled. "So are you."

There was an awkward moment when Madeline stood at the door to say good-night. Tom smiled down at her and thanked her for a wonderful evening. He then leaned down and gave her a long, slow kiss while pulling her close before he turned and walked away.

CHAPTER 36

The regulars were relieved when they found out the killer had been caught. Of course, they all agreed it was so obvious from the beginning that Tony was guilty. They didn't understand why Billy took such a long time to discover what they knew all along.

But nobody was more relieved than Matt. He was thinking maybe, finally, things had turned around for him. He was very surprised when Kate and Samantha met him at the bus one afternoon. Samantha had received a life-insurance payment that would cover his debt, so she told him it was forgiven. Kate finally had come to believe that Matt had been punished enough for his mistake, plus she and the boys missed him. She told him he could come home if he wanted and she would put the divorce on hold, and they would see how things went.

Fern had changed significantly since Roberta's death and Tony's ruin. She found a new and better job, dressed more professionally and no longer let anybody push her around. She redecorated her living room, with all but one of the unicorn pictures removed, and replaced the pillows with a leather sofa and chair.

The biggest change, however, was the bus itself. With all the publicity from the murder showing the dilapidated *bus of death*, the bus company was shamed into finally replacing the old one with a brand-new, clean, well-lit luxury coach with soft seats and working shock absorbers. The interior was a somewhat startling pink and purple swirl of color. As a bonus, it had reliable heating and air conditioning.

* * *

Madeline received what she considered a mysterious call from Tom a week after their dinner at her home. He told her she was to be ready for him to pick her up on Saturday morning at ten sharp and she should wear something that was washable. But he refused to tell her where they were going, only that it would be unforgettable and make her very happy.

They drove for almost an hour with little conversation. When Madeline glanced at him, he was smiling broadly. She became even more curious and nervous. Finally, he turned into a short, pothole-riddled driveway in front of an extremely run-down small motel. The loudly buzzing neon sign read *Lan Mot l o V can s*.

"So, we are here?" Madeline asked dubiously. Tom nodded. She did not know what to think. "I can see why you suggested washable clothing."

They walked to the run-down office, where a tall skinny man with missing teeth came to the door. "Hi, Tom. Great to see you."

"Madeline, this is Archie. He is an old and good friend. Another good man who helped me when I needed it."

"I see that the lady is a little bit nervous, Tom. But that's to be expected under the circumstances." Archie winked at her and gave her a knowing smile. "After all, this is a life-changing experience. Right, Tom?" Tom nodded in agreement.

Tom grabbed Madeline's arm and pulled her along as Archie led them to a door with a *2* painted on it. He turned the key, and the noise began. Six small bundles of fur rushed toward the door, and a much larger one wagged her tail happily.

"Oh, they are sooo cute!" Madeline squealed as she knelt down, and the puppies rushed to her jumping, nipping and licking.

"These are Brittany spaniels. An all-round excellent gun dog, they point and retrieve. And they make great companion animals," Archie explained. "Best dogs ever, in my opinion."

"Archie breeds the finest hunting dogs in Pennsylvania."

"No, Tom, you are dead wrong, there. The best in the whole US of A. I watch my breeding lines like a hawk. These dogs are healthy, sweet tempered, intelligent and beautiful."

"Oh! I want one!"

Tom laughed. "That is why we are here. Losing your detecting skills already?"

Madeline made a face at Tom.

"Pick out any one you want. Or take two. They're small!" Archie said.

She watched the six puppies for a few minutes as they played, and finally she picked up the biggest and fattest male in the litter. "I like this one."

"Well, he has a definite personality that one does. An alpha male if I ever saw one." He glanced at Tom. "But you have another alpha male to help you control him, if I am not mistaken."

The puppy was licking Madeline's face enthusiastically and she was laughing. When she heard this, she glanced at Tom, who was grinning broadly at her.

"Now it's your turn, Tom," Archie said. "But I think Rosie is gonna help you."

Tom was standing apart from the commotion. The mother came up and gave him a sniff, left and returned with a small female following her. They both sat down in front of Tom and stared up at him. Tom smiled and picked up the little dog.

"How much do I owe you, Archie?" Madeline asked.

Archie looked at Tom. "Nothing. It's been taken care of. Just take him home and love him."

"I can definitely do that!" she said while staring into Tom's eyes.

Madeline resumed her Saturday-night habit of eating dinner at The Opossum, but she no longer ate alone sitting at the bar. Now she and Tom shared a table for two.

ACKNOWLEDGEMENTS

I owe particular thanks to the many friends who helped me through the writing process. Pamela Scott Arnold, Paul Landman, and Sam Ruello each read several versions of this book and each gave me thoughtful critiques and encouragement. Betsy DuBois gave the book to her friend, Dr. Ronald Uva, who in turn introduced me to my editor Paul Dinas. Paul worked with me through several rewrites and gave me invaluable advice, while reining in my more frivolous ideas. The Reverend Canon Elizabeth Geitz read the very first version and encouraged me to continue anyway!